RUN FROM HOME

WAY HOME SERIES BOOK THREE

KIM MILLS

❀ Created with Vellum

This book is dedicated to all the soldiers we have walked with who have had to leave the path they started on and face a new one and have managed to make it their own.
And as much, it's dedicated to the ones we have walked with who struggled so fiercely and, in the end, lost their fight.
You have all changed pieces of my heart.

In the end, we will always run back to the one who feels like home.
~ Unknown

PROLOGUE

TWIZ

WINTER 2007

*I*t's far hotter in this bed than it should be.

That's my first thought when I come to consciousness. My room in the condo is always cool, and I sleep with the window open even in the winter. Right now, though, I'm burning up. The blanket covering me is heavy and way too hot. My head feels like there's a ping pong game being played behind my eyelids. I try to scramble together memories about the night before, but nothing seems to stick.

I will myself to peel open my sandpaper eyelids and realize it's not a blanket covering me at all. It's a woman and judging by the soft comforter and purple wall colour, I'm at her place.

She's still asleep, I can feel her rhythmic breathing against my chest. One of her slender arms is thrown across my waist. My naked waist.

I quick glance down and I can see neither of us have anything on. Not that I'd complain about that, she has a slim,

1

KIM MILLS

athletic build with pale, white skin that's dotted with freckles. A redhead. I smile.

I love redheads.

I shift just slightly so I can see her head and confirm my suspicion.

Except I can't. She must be a redhead, but she has nothing but soft stubble on her head. It's shaved completely bald.

That's when the previous night rushes back to me. At the pub, we were meeting in support of Major Lawson's wife who was re-starting her chemo treatments. The women all shaved their heads, Tav's girl Jules, Silas' widow Beth, and two others. Megan's sister, and her best friend. What was her name?

Erika. She was a gorgeous redhead until she sauntered up and asked me to help her shave her head. Then she was just plain gorgeous, even without the hair. The party continued after that. Shots, tequila... I think. Erika went drink for drink with me, not an easy feat since I must outweigh her by almost a hundred pounds and have hard drinking down to an art. She didn't seem any worse for wear than I was, though.

We shared a cab. I remember her pressed up against me in it when we decided to only make one stop. After that, I'm surprised we even made it into her bed. I'm pretty sure we made more than a few pit stops. The hall. The kitchen.

The kitchen table. Even hungover, my body immediately reacts to the memory of spreading her out on that kitchen table. She was exactly what I love in a woman; definitely no passive participant, she more than gave as good as she got.

More than once.

I squeeze my eyes shut a moment and will it all down. It doesn't matter how hot she is, I don't do mornings. Ever. I need to get out of here

It takes me a good five minutes to slowly extract myself from underneath Erika's sleeping form without waking her. It's an art I've mostly perfected, getting out from underneath a

2

woman and on my way before she can wake and ask me for more.

One night, a few laughs, hot sex, and a quick getaway. That's all I ever do. I never promise more, I'm not a monster, I'm always honest that it's just because I don't have more in me to give. This is who I am and what I do. Even sitting as close to thirty as I am, it's never changed. If anything, it's become even more ingrained in me.

I can't give them more when I don't have it in me to give.

This works in my life. And with pre-deployment training coming up and another trip to Afghanistan on the horizon, more than ever a quick exit is the best option. No matter the laughs, or how good the sex.

And holy shit, it was… amazing.

Once I'm off the bed, I take another long moment to enjoy Erika's sleeping figure. She's on her stomach, the blanket sitting just below where her back slopes to her ass. The freckles on her shoulders trail down the slight indent of her spine. I can't see her face since she's got it buried into a pillow, but I find myself smiling at the slightly uneven buzz cut, a few errant strands still hang in a few places.

I won't be giving up my day job to take up as a barber, apparently.

Grabbing my jeans and t-shirt from the night before, I can smell booze and a woman's scent lingering on them as I slip into them as quietly as I can and attempt to soften the click when I open the door.

"Ah… Twiz was it?" I hear muffled behind me.

Shit.

I turn, bracing myself for the inevitable 'you asshole sneaking out without saying goodbye' lecture. Instead, Erika rolls onto her back, not bothering to pull up the blanket, and I'm the one almost convinced to stay at the sight in front of me.

"Ya?"

"Hit the button on the coffee maker on the way out, would ya?" She waves one hand in the direction of the door before rolling again to the side and closing her eyes.

It's sheer mechanics that gets me down the hall and into the kitchen where I find a pre-set coffee maker. I press the button and head out, taking only a final glance at that kitchen table before I close the door behind me.

Huh.

The one woman who doesn't seem to care to see me walk out the door in the morning and for the first time in as long as I can remember, I almost want to stay.

TWIZ

SPRING 2009

*I*t's like we've been in this desert for years.

Well, if I think about all the time I've spent here, I guess altogether it has been close. The heat, the smell, the dust... it doesn't even seem wrong anymore, mostly just seems routine. Tired. Old.

Never thought I'd say it, but it's getting old.

This is my third deployment to the same country in six years. I'm almost in my twentieth month here. Six years ago, I was here as a corporal, excited for the opportunity. Now, I'm their sergeant. Some days I'm happy for the position, for how well I've done, for the chance to lead and make a difference.

Other days, I wonder how I could possibly take these lives into my hands. The responsibility isn't one I take lightly, it weighs on me every moment I am here. These aren't just my teammates like they have been before. These are my soldiers. My platoon. Bringing them home is my only end game.

We have a week left. I've never been so happy, so relieved

while at the same time jealous. Watching the guys' excitement ramp up as we get closer and closer to going home to family is bittersweet. It's just me at home, if by home I mean the townhouse I share with Matt. Which is a step up to every other deployment when I came home to an empty, cement-walled, shared-bathroom room on base.

Looks like I am growing up a little. Might rub that in the face of that last girl I slept with... Mona? Mora? Mira? Who knows. I do know she told me when I went to leave, exactly like I told her I would, that I would never change. I'd give her an 'I told you so,' but I won't see her again, so I guess it doesn't matter.

There's no woman at home waiting for me, as much as whatshername thought she wanted to be. Matt will probably even cut out for a few weeks to visit family, too. Which is fine, we've been under each other's feet for months now. A little distance won't hurt.

What I have to look forward to is my own bed and whatever warm and willing body I decide to share it with for a night.

I'm not complaining.

It's life exactly how I designed it.

"Sarg..." The flap on the tent bursts open, and Matt glances inside quickly and sees we're alone when he drops the formality. "Twiz. I need you out here. We have an Op, orders in five."

I sit up from the bunk I lay on, stretching my arms out from under my head. I grab my rifle and sling it over my shoulder and follow him out.

A week left is still a week of work, no matter how many daydreams of home.

A half hour later, the orders are given out and we sit in prime hurry up and wait position, just holding off for our final go ahead. There's some intel of insurgents in a town nearby, and we'll be heading in with the translators and local forces to do a little housecleaning.

I won't be going into the town so much as hanging out on the outskirts with my rifle, on overwatch. Without a sniper team with us, I'll be sharpshooter for the Op, up on slightly higher ground. I've gotten comfortable with it over these months, looking over my platoon and the others with us, from a distance, taking out dangers before they get too close.

We'll head in all as a group and then I'll take Tav with me to find my spot. Quick set up and I can watch over the platoons. It's routine, really, we've cleared through so many towns, a bunch of them more than once. There's always some intel, whether it's someone hiding out or someone building bombs or just another kid hoping to trade vague stories for a few bucks or a move to another town. We're just the follow-up team.

We get the green light and head past the wire. Tav falls in step next to me.

"Master Corporal Cleary! How's married life?" I've been asking him the same question every day for the almost eight months of this deployment. The exact same way, because ever since he was promoted just months before we left, I like to remind him.

"Hasn't changed since you asked me yesterday, fucker. Ask me again when I'm home in bed with my woman under me my first night back and you're stuck still sleeping alone a few feet from the captain. I've heard that man snore."

"Whatever. I bet Jules snores like an elephant."

Tav gives me a quick shove. "Fuck off. And even if she did, she comes with a hell of a lot more perks. I'll listen to her snore every night if it means I get to sleep next to her the rest of my life."

"Wait. Wait, I don't think I can roll my eyes far enough back for that level of bullshit. You, brother, are completely whipped."

He just smiles, and he knows that despite it all, I'm happy for him. It's not been an easy road. More than a couple of us had our eyes on him coming back to this sandbox, worried he'd end up in a bad place again after what happened on the last tour with Silas. But so far, he's been just fine, and I'm glad because he's not only my brother, he's a damn fine soldier that I'm relieved to keep on our team.

Still, all that romantic bullshit gets a little old.

We get quieter as we get closer. The loudest noise is Tav clenching and unclenching his fists. It's his nervous tic, let's me know his adrenaline is kicking in.

I know because I have made it part of my job to know. I know the tics of all my soldiers. Tav with his fist clenching. Matt chews his bottom lip. Our old boss, Major Lawson, he cracked everything—fingers, neck, wrists. One of my master corporals, VanHerse, he grinds his teeth.

Everyone has one. Most are all variations of the same things. Except our youngest private on this deployment, Carson. He sings, barely there quiet under his breath. Mostly *Phantom of the Opera*. That's a new one for me.

I'm not immune. I have my own, they're just internal. Years of quiet observation, of sitting for hours trying to keep a steady hand, and I've moved all my nervous tics to the inside. Mostly, I count. I count steps. Count cars. Count people. Count seconds. The fact no one can see it makes me look much less wound up than everyone around me, unflappable, unmoving. That's exactly how I like it. My cards aren't just close to my chest, they're buried deep inside it.

Knowing their tics, however, comes in handy; I can then use them to see more. Like right now, when Tav stops for a second before cracking his knuckles and holding his fist even tighter.

He feels something off. Not enough that he's said anything yet, but his tic gives him away and gives me an advantage. My eyes dart faster. He's right, something IS off.

I nod to him and we silently make our way a little higher to the top of the embankment. The platoons are below us, the interpreter talking to some village elders. Everything looks fine but that doesn't change the fact that Tav's knuckles are whiter each time he clenches his fists.

I click my radio. "Two, this is Two-One Alpha. Set."

"Rog'r," Captain Christiansen, who on a regular day is my roommate Matt, but right now is the 2IC, responds in my ear.

Fifty-two, fifty-three, fifty-four... my mind counts breaths, the sound of Tav's knuckles, the sand under our feet. From my rifle scope I see off to the side, a woman, barely old enough to need the hijab dwarfing her head, break from a small group of locals on the side of the road. She keeps stepping closer to the men who have started their conversation with the local elders.

Fifty-nine, sixty... I see how the scarf on her head meets her chest. It's bulky. Too bulky for someone her size. I glance back to her face. She's not just young, she's... she's confused. She keeps nervously looking behind her. Her head sways a little back and forth. It only takes a second to see it. She's got a delay, a mental handicap that's clear when I watch her as she moves with the steps of a child. Someone has told her to walk towards the platoon, and she doesn't want to do it. Her constant checks back confirm it. I click to my radio.

"Two-One, this is Two-One Alpha. Contact sector Alpha. Suspicious girl, brown hijab, moving south towards Cpl. Goudreau."

"Seen," Lt. Froese's voice answers and I see him take a step in her direction but she's already closing in on one of the other corporals, a young Newfie named JC.

Seventy-seven, seventy-eight... JC notices her approach and says something in English while putting his hand out in a motion to tell her to stop. She only cocks her head even more confused and keeps moving. Lt. Froese calls to him, but JC can't hear. He yells to her now, most likely to stop, before turning to get the interpreter's attention. As soon as his head turns, though, it seems to disappear, a mist of blood in its place as he falls. The bullet hit just above his vest into his neck. The panic I see in the group now is a physical thing, I can feel it from here.

"FUCK, where did that come from?" Tav is next to me, moving his rifle to every conceivable hiding spot, looking for the shooter. I stay fixed on the woman. There are tears running down her face now, and her steps falter, but she moves forward still, slowly towards the men who have jumped to ready positions. Matt's attention is turned, now the radio is blowing up with calls for backup, medics, and a chopper.

"Fucker." Tav's voice has lost the urgent edge, and I know it's because he's in the black, completely focused now. He's found the shooter. His rifle fires.

"Got him." He starts to move.

"Wait." I say in barely a whisper and he crouches next to me, looking through his own scope.

"You think she is rigged?" he asks as he follows my gaze to the girl who continues to walk amid the panicked locals and fight-ready soldiers around her. She's headed to where JC has fallen, where there are soldiers all around, presumably to give first aid and move him out. The lieutenant is still on the radio for a helicopter. Her steps are slow. Deliberate.

Ninety-nine, one hundred, one hundred and one... "She's headed for the medic."

I see the shift in her shoulders and the bulk under her scarves moves just enough. It's clear what's there. Tavish sees it too.

"Take the shot." I don't look at Tav. His voice is still calm, detached. He knows what needs to be done. He hates it as much as I do, but not as much as I know I will.

When my rifle fires, and she goes down, I drop my head and notice before I stand the taste of blood from where I've been biting my tongue.

2

ERIKA

*N*o matter how long I stare at this computer screen, it won't get any more interesting.

So many years at this company and nothing changes. I've been in this same office since I graduated college, doing the same work. At least now I feel like I've earned it, instead of that twenty-year-old college grad who got the office manager job because her dad is the boss.

Not the best way to make friends.

I tap a deep-red acrylic nail on the side of my monitor and stare blankly. It's only one p.m. Time is going so slowly. The sad part is, once I'm done here, I have nothing more exciting to do. A stop at the gym on the way home from work. A glass of wine and some of the soup I made earlier in the week, in front of bad TV. Then bed, up for a run at six tomorrow. Happy Friday night.

I'm in a rut. A really boring rut.

I glance over outside my office door to the desk where my best friend used to sit. Megan left last summer with her military husband for Ottawa, leaving me stuck here alone. Again. Megan was really the only friend I'd made, and now in her place, is a perfectly nice, middle-aged woman named Donna, with her trendy haircut and her Friday baking for the staff room. She's delightful. But she's not Megan and I miss my friend. I was never good at making them and without her, I don't even know where to start again.

My computer dings with an email, and I delete it without even opening it. I can tell by the subject I know who it's from. I shudder. That wasn't what I was hoping for when I was wishing for excitement.

It should bother me more, but I've been getting the same skeevy emails, phone calls, letters from him for years. Years. I'm sure I should still be scared but I'm not the naive, insecure seventeen-year-old girl he tried to break, I'm closer to thirty these days and he doesn't terrify me anymore. Now when he pops up occasionally, he only pisses me off. I'm always quick to ignore him, thinking maybe he'll go away. I should do more, I'm sure, but I don't. I can't control him, but I can control my response. And so far, that response is pretending it's not happening.

Sure, it's been a decade, but I'm convinced one of these days, he'll get the hint.

So, instead of dealing with it, I head to the washroom and take a good, long look in the mirror. I'm the only one in here, which is good because it gives me a moment to run my hands up and down where my shirt hits my slacks and feel the little bump that needs to be worked on. I turn around to see how my ass is falling slightly, probably because I've been focusing a little more on upper body at the gym. I make a mental note that must change. Holding my arms up and waving them, the tiny jiggle is just what I need to motivate me to add an extra few kilometers to the training run tomorrow. I can control all of this, and I take a deep breath, knowing I've got it. I have goals and I know I'll achieve them. I'm good.

Back in my office, the hours pass slowly as day nears its end.

I take a quick trip down the hallway for my dreaded but necessary visit with Dad. He is the boss, so that means I give him numbers and projections and all that comes with that most days. Which makes him deliriously happy; this way, he can be sure that I literally cannot make it through my days without him.

I knock on the glass beside his open door. My dad is at his desk, head bent, the shine of the skin on the top seeming to reflect the light from the window right out the door. His desk is littered with papers and the supplies I ensure he has, because he wouldn't even know where the Staples catalogue is. There's only one photo on the cluttered bookcase to his right, of him and me at my high school graduation. He's beaming next to me while I'm mostly just staring at the diploma in my hands. The picture is a decade old and I hate it because I'm a good fifty pounds overweight, my face rounded and my shape pushing against the limits of the sleeves of my too small graduation gown. I try to take it down all the time, but Dad insists it's his favourite.

I even framed a photo of me at the finish line of the last marathon I ran, hoping it would replace this one but of course, he only smiled and left it at home, hidden somewhere. I've never seen it since.

"Hi, sweetheart." Dad smiles up at me. That's another thing he won't change, even at work. He insists on calling me pet names like it's not already bad enough that I'm his daughter and his office manager.

"Hi, Dad." I walk in and place today's paperwork on top of the paperwork I had given him yesterday that still isn't filed. If I moved enough around on this desk, I bet I'd find all the papers for this week. I make a mental note to come in and clean up in here Monday.

"What are your plans for this weekend, honey?" He's fishing, I know he is, but I don't have the patience to really care.

13

"I'm going to head to the gym and then it's an early night for me, I have a long run in the morning." Marathon training is no joke, and I'm always marathon training. I have a couple of races on the books for this summer and fall, and I'll probably add more.

"I wish you'd take a break from all that, Erika. You're so skinny and always running everywhere..." Dad trails off. He hates the training. Probably because it's less time I can spend out for dinner with him, or watching sports with him, or, well, basically anything that involves me always being with him.

"I'm not skinny, Dad. I'm just not fat. Why don't you come by for brunch on Sunday?" If I don't invite him to something, he'll just end up popping in and last time he did that, I had a very cute, very young college student in a very small towel in my kitchen, making us breakfast. Since then, I do my best to make sure there's no surprise visits.

His face lights up. "That sounds great, sweetie."

I head back to my office and grab my purse, saying goodbye as the rest of the staff leaves for the day before closing. My baby, Bethany, sits in the far end of the parking lot, a fire-engine red, 1976 Camaro. Not the baby most women envision as they slide into their thirties, but this one couldn't be more perfect. I got in on a police auction while dating an officer a few years ago and knew she would be mine the moment I saw her.

That's saying something, too. I live in Alberta, so she only really sees the outside less than half the year; the rest of the time, my beat-up F-150 is what gets me around in the cold.

Still, though, Bethany makes me deliriously happy, and I feel the stress melt as soon as I sit in the driver's seat and turn her over. If I'm going to commute from downtown, I might as well enjoy it. Besides, it's not like I have any car seats or sticky toddlers to worry about. Thank goodness.

I pull my hair out of the small bun at the back of my head and run my fingers through it a few times. It's still damp at the crown from this morning's shower and shaking it out helps to relieve even more of the tension sitting behind my eyelids. It still hasn't reached a good length since I shaved it with Megan when she re-started chemo for breast cancer about a year ago, but at least I can pull it back now.

I pull up at the gym a few blocks from home and grab my bag from the back. I just started here last month when I decided to take on an obstacle course race as part of my schedule this summer. Running, I can do. Monkey bars? Not so much. So, I've been hitting some weight training classes in the afternoons. It's not my favourite; I'd honestly rather just lace my shoes and run ten kilometers, but I'm here.

A girl must have goals, right?

Especially when she doesn't have a whole lot else going on. The gym is the perfect distraction and it's easy to make the goals and complete them. It's like a game, and I'm always winning.

I walk in, scanning the tag on my keychain, and head to the locker room. Pulling off the pencil skirt, blouse, and bra is almost freeing, until I wrestle into my sports bra and Lulus. I throw a quick t-shirt over and head out in my bare feet to the kickboxing class I signed up for.

This is the first of this class, a new session advertised by the gym as a fitness class combined with women's self-defence. Surprisingly, it is offered for free here and so I jumped to register, figuring it would be a good chance to see if I liked it before I paid for the cardio-kickboxing classes they usually run with the same instructor. The self-defence part? Sure, why not? Better late than never.

I'm the first one in and I sit on the mat and stretch when I see another pair of bare feet enter. It must be an instructor, since these are male feet. I glance up and see that he has his back to me as other participants enter the small room. I let my gaze travel slowly up his form and admire the view. He's wearing loose gym shorts low on his hips, muscular calves on display. Covering his back is a funny-coloured, like a deep maroon t-shirt, which makes me pause a moment until I see the military symbol between the shoulder blades. Living here next to an Army base, I see a lot of military types. I've dated more than a few, none ever really kept my attention, even after Megan up and married one. Truth be told, there's so many around, they barely catch a second glance from me anymore. This one, however, has my attention. I can see his biceps straining past the short sleeves of the shirt and out from his back that even under the fabric, I can tell is thickly muscled. There are dark, menacing-looking tattoos snaking out and down his forearm. They look like tree branches, black and foreboding, the kind that scare you when they rattle against your window at night. They look almost familiar, and I find myself focused on them, trying to place where I've seen them before.

Suddenly, the music starts and before I can turn away and hide my obvious stare, he turns around.

Shit.

SHIT.

I know even before I see his eyes. I'd remember them anywhere because they're hard to forget. One blue, one brown. And that can only mean one thing.

I've slept with my instructor.

He was the one who was at Megan's head-shaving party before she re-started chemo. Ryan? Richard? I don't remember his first name, but I remember what they were calling him.

Twiz.

It's too late to look away now so I hold his gaze and I see the moment he, too, realizes I'm not a stranger. If he has trouble placing where he's met me, he hides it well. He drops his eyes a moment, and I can feel them travelling my body the same way mine just travelled his, before he looks back to my face with a smirk.

I've slept with my share of one-night stands without shame, and it's not like I've never bumped into one before, but this one is different. This one I don't just remember his face.

I remember everything. And it was good.

Like, filed away for later, good. Surpassed all the other ones before and since good. The kind of good I've spent more than one night alone remembering.

That makes this so much more awkward, since I'm sure I was just another notch on his already filled-up bedpost. I doubt he has any toys in his nightstand named after me.

Not that, you know, I do…

I try to keep my features neutral as I catch his eye and wink. I can play this cool. That's what I do. I mean, I'm not some blushing virgin that he can catch off guard and make me stutter, and there's no way I'm giving him the satisfaction of thinking I am.

"Erika, right?" He steps towards me, his voice smooth and a frustratingly perfect smirk on his face.

"Good memory," I answer. He only smiles wider.

"It sure is a good memory." He's not even trying to hide his blatant sexual undertone now, and I find myself swallowing under his gaze, hoping it goes unnoticed, but I watch his eyes drop to my throat.

Fine, two can play at this game.

"Sure, I guess it was, but my memory seems to be fading. Ryan, was it?"

His eyes flit back to mine and his smile falters for only a half second. If I wasn't staring so intently, I wouldn't have even noticed. Then he only smiles wider. It's a cocky smile, and it reminds me of the confidence that got me into this mess in the first place. He has no doubts.

"You remember my name."

He says it with finality, and then backs up until he's at the front of the group that's now gathered all around. I see another man in the corner, slightly smaller, wearing one of the gym logo shirts with a pair of loose jogging shorts.

"Hi everyone, my name is Rob, but generally I answer to Twiz. Don't ask, I promise it's not as interesting a story as you think it is. I'll be teaching the self-defence portion of this class, along with Shane here who will be helping me and taking you through the fitness aspects. He's a personal trainer here and an instructor on several other classes this gym offers. The two of us have taught this course a few times at this gym, and I'm looking forward to our next several weeks together.

"As for myself, I have a brown belt in Brazilian Jiu Jitsu and have trained as well in Judo and Muay Thai kickboxing. For this class, however, a lot of what I'll be teaching comes from what I've learned in the military as a CQC, or Close Quarter Combat, instructor. I know that can sound a little intimidating but let me just be clear. I'm not teaching anyone to be a fighter. What I will teach is the best techniques to get yourself out of a situation, so you can get away. Running, getting to safety, will always be the primary goal. Does anyone have any questions?"

One woman in the back, a heavier lady probably in her mid-forties, raises her hand and calls out. "Are you in the military still, or do you work here?" She looks like she's ready to bolt, for whatever reason, and Twiz beams a smile at her that makes her blush, disarming her whole appearance. Just because he can.

"I am in the military. I'm a sergeant in the infantry. I don't work here. I'm just here as a volunteer, to help out."

"Why?" The question is out of my mouth before I can think it through.

"It's just something I like to do," Twiz answers, looking away quickly to our other instructor, who gives us instructions for a warm up. Soon, I'm caught up in burpees and jumping jacks until I notice Twiz counting us off from the front. He works his way through the group, pairing people of similar size off until he is standing right in front of me.

"Well, Erika, it looks like an odd-numbered group. Will you be okay partnered up with me?" He's smiling when he says it, but I can see by the look on his face, he truly means the question. I can tell he knows that, for some women in the class, working with a man would be hard, scary even. I wonder if there's a real reason he's here teaching.

"Sure, Twiz, that should be fine. Thank you."

I don't know if it will be fine, but damned if I'm going to let him think he intimidates me. He just gives me that same half-assed grin and heads back to the front of the class.

True to his word, nothing he teaches is terribly difficult or demanding. Starting with basic posture and defence from a standing position, I pick up a few tricks. I'm only maybe three or four inches shorter than he is, though significantly lighter, and all his demonstrations happen at arm's length. We barely have to touch at all and when we do, it's only for a moment before I practice a throw or an escape.

I convince myself I am not disappointed about this.

When cool down comes to an end, I pick myself up off the sweaty mat and head towards the locker room when I hear my name from behind.

"Erika. Hold up." Twiz bounds up to me from the front, his towel in his hand, his own sweat making his shirt cling to his chest in a way that is almost unfair. His eyes catch mine, seeking them out and leading them up. It's funny how at first, it's almost like I can't place what his eye colour is. I try to describe him to someone and it just seems off, that I can't remember what his eyes looked like. Then I look closer to realize they're both completely different. Not slightly variant shades, but two distinct colours, bright blue and deep brown. It's disarming how unique it makes him look, especially with his black hair and light skin.

"I hope that was all okay. I'd be really disappointed if you left the class because of me." The look on his face is nothing but honest, and it surprises me. I would think he'd be happy if I just quietly disappeared.

"Yeah, Twiz, it was fine. I can't say I was expecting to see you, but it's cool. I'm going to stay in the class. Really, it's no big deal. And you're a great teacher. You obviously know your stuff." I give an almost honest smile back. It wasn't a big deal; the class was great. The only thing that makes it all a lie is the heat I feel every time he's nearby and I don't know if he even notices.

"Good. Good. I'd... I wouldn't mind seeing you again."

I look at him a moment. He looks about as confused as I do at what just came out of his mouth.

"You didn't strike me as a repeat kind of guy."

"I'm not." He shrugs.

"It's probably better that way." I give him a smile and turn into the girl's change room. I make absolutely, a hundred percent sure not to look back.

No matter how badly I want to.

3

TWIZ

*D*amn, that woman fueled more fantasies in the desert than an entire Playboy roster, and she only looks better in person.

I've been teaching these classes with Shane ever since he left the military and started the whole personal trainer gig. He ran the idea by me when he started at the gym, so whenever I'm in town, I volunteer for the eight-week class as a self-defence instructor alongside him. I'm not sure why he knew I'd be in for something like that, but not a lot of guys have the qualifications I do. I jumped at the chance. I get a little shot at self-redemption once a week while I teach basic self-defence to women for free, and through it, he gets more registrations for his other classes.

I never considered, when he asked if I'd be up for this, that I'd see Erika my first day. I've thought of that woman almost constantly since our night together, even when it's been over a year now.

That kitchen table of hers has starred in a whole lot of bedtime stories.

I throw my sweaty towel in my gym bag and grab my hoodie

from my locker, zipping it up over my gym clothes. I'm just heading straight back to my place from here, so I don't bother showering. I tell myself it's not because I'm rushing to see Erika one more time on her way out, but it doesn't matter because I don't. Waving to Shane who's already with another client at the weights, I head out to my Silverado and home.

The townhouse I share with Matt looks more and more every day that it's lived in by a couple of lazy bachelors, and I can't even blame Matt. I dropped him at the airport last week so he could use his post-deployment leave to visit his parents. This mess of unopened mail, dirty dishes, and laundry everywhere is all me. Along with the line of empty Golden Wedding and Black Velvet bottles on the counter.

You can take the boy out of the country, but he brings his redneck drinks with him.

Truth is we only grew up and got a place off base about a year ago. Matt decided he wanted to buy somewhere, so once he settled on this place, he asked if I'd want to come rent with him to help with the mortgage. Probably also because I don't think either of us has ever lived completely alone, and the idea seems a little strange. Whatever the reason, one or both of us is gone more than half the time anyway so it seems to work.

My phone rings before I even make it out of the shower. I know the phone I bought when I got home has a keyboard; the guy at the counter was very excited to show me. I, however, don't want to write to people. If I have something to say I can say it aloud and my friends know it. They finally stopped trying to send text messages and they just call me.

Sometimes I even answer.

Communication has never been my strong suit.

It doesn't surprise me that Mike's number pops up. Even though he left the Army shortly after we got back in 2007, he and I have managed to keep in touch. He even came out and met me when I was on leave. Now, I've been back less than two weeks, but I haven't seen him yet. I'm sure that's what this is about. I don't have any plans tonight anyways, so why not?

"Hey, Twiz!" He's yelling far louder than necessary into the phone, which makes me glance at the clock. I guess it's almost eight. Still... seems a little early to be in the yelling drunk phase.

The noise in the background gives him away.

"Don't tell me you're at Silvers?" I ask about the dance club downtown usually filled with teenagers and college students. He laughs into the phone, and I hold it away from my ear.

"Hell ya!"

"A little old for that shit, aren't we?"

I turned thirty while I was in the sandbox and I don't know if it was the age or just the amount of time I've spent dodging bullets... maybe it's just all the sand-induced wrinkles. Whatever it is, I feel too damn old for the pick-up bars these days.

Mike just laughs. "Ya man, we probably are. But I've met some lovely ladies and lucky for your old ass, they wanted to find somewhere a bit quieter. And since there's two of them..."

He makes me laugh. He'd have no trouble with two, but maybe he figures his odds are better if I take the friend out of the picture.

"Mike..."

"One is a seriously hot redhead..." Hmm, he knows how I feel about redheads. One in particular these days, but since she was right, I don't do repeats, I really should find myself an alternative. I haven't gotten laid since I arrived home. That's already out of character for me. Maybe that's why I can't stop thinking about her... I just need to find some suitable distractions.

"Meet you at the usual pub, then?"

"See you in twenty!"

I laugh as I hang up. I guess I'm not that old.

When I arrive, Mike isn't there yet, so I head up to the bar.

"Hey, Jer." I sit and Jeremy, the bartender slash owner, gives me a head nod and pours me a whiskey and coke.

I met Jeremy after we got back in 2007, when we came to visit Tav's girl Juliette. He was retired infantry. Turns out he had even served with our old OC. While we hadn't met him when he'd been in, he became one of us fast. And since the group of us is here more often than not, we've gotten to know him really well.

"Twiz, here on your own?" I give a look around. It's busy, but for a Friday night, that's to be expected. I catch a glimpse of Tav's girl as she takes an order at a booth at the back of the bar. That can only mean one thing… I grin when it takes me no time at all to find Tavish at a table nearby, eyes glued to her.

Fucker is so predictable.

"I was. Mike's on his way and looks like Tav is at his usual spot." I grab my drink from Jeremy, who's already moved on to more orders, and walk over to Tavish's table to sit.

"You're so pussy whipped."

He doesn't even move his eyes to my direction.

"Yup."

For a moment, when I see her face light up as she catches his eyes on the way to type in the order, I'm almost jealous. After losing Silas, and then the shitshow that ended our last Op this past tour, it's been more than clear to the rest of us that Jules is his peace. I can see his hand, fidgeting the ring on his finger for just a moment before it stills. Tavish's tells don't consume him this go around, not like the last time. Sure, shit is hard and that won't change, but he's dealing this time. Not even going to lie and pretend we weren't snooping more than a little to be sure— we definitely were. We came far too close to losing him the first time, so the way he's adjusting this time? I must give at least some of that credit to Jules.

He looks back at me with a measure of sympathy I wasn't expecting.

"You doing all right?" he asks in the way only he can because only he knows. We've never spoken about what happened on overwatch that day. There's nothing to say. I took the shot because it needed to be taken. I probably saved the lives of a few of our guys on the ground. He was there, though, so unlike the others that saw only the aftermath and the safety it gave, he knows what it really cost.

Not much.

Just her life, and my peace.

It takes me a moment to answer, and I notice his gaze trail to my jaw. I realize I'm biting my tongue between my eyetooth and the one below. I move it, quick, but it's too late. He's seen it.

"Twiz, if you need..." He is cut off by the booming sound of Mike's drunken voice through the bar.

"Twiz! We're heeeeere!"

"For fuck's sake, Mike, no one cares. Keep it down or I'll throw your ass out before you sit!" Jeremy calls, only half-joking from the bar.

Mike just grins. "Sorry, man."

He's not sorry.

He has a couple of girls with him, one seems to somehow have one of her hands plastered in his back pocket, which takes some serious maneuvering on her part as he sways his way towards us. The other walks a few steps behind, her head down as she looks for something in her purse. When she looks up, she uses a hand to push her short, red hair from her face and stops in her tracks.

Holy crap. A giant smile spreads across my face.

"Well, hello, Erika," I say and stand, moving one of the chairs next to me out so she can sit.

"Twiz." She cocks her head to the side and I can practically see the wheels in her head turning as she tries to decide if she thinks I planned this.

"Hey, don't look at me. Mike only told me he was bringing a

hot redhead with him. He didn't give me any names!" I hold my hands out in mock surrender. She shakes her head and takes a seat. Juliette is there quickly, and I ask Erika what I can order for her.

"Absolutely nothing, but I'll order myself a soda water if you could, Juliette."

"You really should let me buy you a drink," I say once Jules is gone with everyone's orders in hand.

"I buy my own drinks." There's a finality in her voice that reminds me she was in my self-defence class just hours earlier, and I shut my mouth.

"Fair enough. So, girls' night?"

I glance over at Mike and the brunette he came in with. The girl is practically sitting on his lap as she giggles and plays with the buttons on his shirt.

"I work with Andrea and she called, convinced me we were just going out for a drink or two. By the time I realized that wasn't really the plan, she had hooked up with this guy. I didn't want to send her off alone with some stranger." I look at her for a moment, assessing. She buys her own drinks. She won't let her friend go off with a guy, even though it's clear with her straight back and sparkling water, she's not interested in a night on the town.

She's smart and a good friend, but I can't help but think there might be more.

"Well, while I'm not saying Mike isn't a complete idiot, I will vouch that he's a harmless idiot. Your friend will be safe with him."

She looks over at the couple and nods as Jules brings us our drinks.

"Ya, I think I'll just finish my water and head home."

"Awww, don't leave!" Mike slurs from across the table. "If Twiz isn't up for the challenge, you can always join the two of us! I promise, I can handle you both!" He winks at her and I hear a low, growling noise.

Holy shit, that came from me.

Mike glances at me and then laughs. I catch a glance at Tav who's smiling hard, too. Dammit.

Erika looks at me quizzically. "I thought you said he was a safe guy."

"He is. Just not for you."

"Oh?" She smiles seductively. "And you are?"

"Stay awhile and you can see."

This time she laughs.

"I think I've already caught that show. And we've established it's a one-time viewing kind of deal."

I shrug non-committedly as though she didn't just say the same thing I've been reminding myself all night, and instead, start asking her more about herself. Pretty soon, I've managed to get her a little more comfortable, and I find myself relaxing into the conversation, though she still hasn't taken off her jacket.

"What are your plans this weekend?"

"I'm training for a race in the fall, so I'm up early for a run. I should actually get going." She grabs some cash from her purse. I'm not sure what she thinks she's paying for since I guarantee Jules isn't charging her for soda water from the tap, but I say nothing.

"Oh ya? I can run. Where are you running?" She looks at me a while before answering, and I let her, giving her the chance to decide if she trusts my company. Finally, she seems to decide that she does. I hate myself a little for how happy that makes me.

"The river valley. Starting right by the conference center."

I go to take a drink of my whiskey, but she puts her hand over mine and pushes it back to the table before handing me a paper from her purse with what looks like her number.

"It's eighteen kilometers. And I'll be there for six forty-five."

With that, she smiles and stands, walking out of the bar without looking back.

Fuck.

Guess I'm going for a run tomorrow.

4

ERIKA

J have no idea what I was thinking; I don't even like running with a partner.

Yet here I am, combing out my hair at some ridiculous, too-early time in the morning on the off chance Twiz decides to join me.

Usually, my runs are my time. I pump the music and retreat in my head, concentrate on the trail under my feet, sure that I get enough air in my lungs. It's freeing, quiet, and I'm the only one that can judge me while I'm out there.

I'm my own harshest critic, but at least it's only my own voice in my head while I'm out.

I climb into Bethany and head down to the valley. The drive downtown this early in the morning on a Saturday is deserted, and it takes me no time at all to pull into the lot next to the trail. There's only a handful of cars here and most I recognize. I might not know the owners, but it's always the same people parked here at this time. Only so many of us are crazy enough to be on the trails this early when the rest of the city sleeps in.

There's one I haven't seen before though, and it stands out because it's a ridiculously oversized, shiny, silver truck. A

Silverado extended cab, and a new one at that. I shake my head when I realize this would be exactly what I would expect Twiz to drive. As I step out, that's confirmed when I see him leaning against the front in a pair of loose basketball shorts and that same faded maroon-coloured shirt he had on yesterday.

I take a moment as I grab my water belt and Garmin, to admire his form as he stretches with a foot up on his truck bumper. I mean, I've seen all of it up close and personal already but with his calves flexing and biceps stretching the sleeves of his t-shirt, he never stops being impressive. He's all lean muscle, clearly in phenomenal shape since he agreed to an eighteen-kilometer run with no warning. However, it's a more unassuming strength than some of the guys like Megan's husband Mark and Juliette's husband Tavish. Those guys are big, imposing looking from first glance, while Twiz takes a second look. It would be easy to be disarmed by the odd colouring of his eyes and his boyish smirk and never really appreciate the strength and muscle under the clothes.

I'm appreciating, though. And when he looks over, I know I've been busted. Again.

Dammit.

He gives me that same infuriating smirk that make my heart jump and walks over.

"Whoa… what's this?" He pats a hand on Bethany's roof while slowly walking around to admire her.

"She is Bethany. She's my baby."

"'75?"

"She's a '76. Picked her up at a police auction a while back."

He whistles and peeks in the open driver's side door.

"I'm impressed. She's in great shape." He stands back up and looks at me. "Why Bethany?"

"She looks like a Bethany, obviously."

He shakes his head and laughs but doesn't argue, which makes me smile. Instead of letting him see, I duck my head and finish strapping the watch on and set it to start. I close the car door and tuck the key in the tiny pocket at the top of my running shorts. When I look up, I catch his eyes fixed on the strip of skin that was exposed while I did.

I grin. Good, at least I'm not the only one getting caught gawking today.

"Ready?"

"I was born ready, babe." I groan, and he laughs at his cheesy response as we head down to the opening of the trail.

"You set the pace, I'll just try to keep up." He sweeps his hand towards the trail. I set off slowly to warm up, the brisk air cooling my lungs for a moment as my breathing picks up. I didn't connect my music today since I was running with a partner, and it's a new experience. The sounds of our feet on the trail and the breeze in the air are the only noise next to our breaths.

"So, Erika, what drives someone to run eighteen kilometers this early on a Saturday morning?" Twiz keeps pace easily beside me, and I'm a little jealous of the way he talks like the run doesn't require any energy at all.

"I have a few races that I've planned in the next while, including the Edmonton marathon in the middle of August and an obstacle race in September. Eighteen kilometers is actually a relatively short run for my training schedule."

He takes a moment to respond, "Marathon runner, eh? Impressive. A few years back, I did the Mountain Man and to be honest, it was not my favourite time."

"What's a Mountain Man?"

"An Army thing. We carry our Ruck and do a thirty-two-kilometer race, followed by three point two kilometers carrying our canoe, then ten-kilometers paddling, then a five point six kilometer run. It happens right down here every year. I've been in Afghanistan or training for Afghanistan most years since then, so I've only done it once. And I'm not complaining."

"Holy shit. That's… impressive." He laughs.

"I suppose, but honestly, I think it's a soldier's trait to keep going when most sane people would stop."

Now it's my turn to laugh.

"So, you're basically saying you're not crazy or impressively fit. You're just stubborn."

"Well, how about we go with a little of both?" He grins, and I shake my head.

"Well no one will accuse you of being humble I suppose."

"Hey, I'm just honest!"

We run for a long while in silence, and I find that while I usually would miss the music in my ears, with him beside me, I enjoy the sounds of the trail. When we hit the Port-O-Potties that mark the turn-around point, we take a short break and each duck into the bathroom before stretching at a bench overlooking the river.

"So, how has it been, coming home?" I ask. We had spoken briefly about how he had just finished another deployment to Afghanistan, but he hadn't really said anything. Having been close to Megan while Mark had been gone and back twice, I know it's not always as easy as they like to make it seem.

"It's colder," he deadpans and then changes the subject, asking about past races I've done. I let his obvious avoidance of the subject go. It's not like I have the right to quiz him on something so personal. Instead, we chat easily about work, training, and cars and before I know it, I can see the parking lot with our vehicles up ahead.

As we round a final corner, I catch glimpse of a dark plastic bag caught in the brush on the side of the trail. I don't even have a chance to register what's happening before both Twiz and I are on the ground, his body over mine, his eyes on the bag. His breath comes in pants and his heart pounds hard enough that I can feel it where his chest is pressed against mine. He blinks a few times and then slowly pulls himself up and off me, sitting back on his heels beside me.

"I... huh. I'm sorry..." He chuckles softly but I can see on his face he's only trying to cover up his embarrassment. I look over at the small bag that's loudly flapping in the breeze, caught on a branch. A piece of broken plastic some squatters or bush partiers probably left behind before the wind stuck it there. I try to see it from his perspective, to imagine the threat but I can't see it. Everything in me wants to comfort him somehow, let him know it's okay, but I don't know how.

He looks like he might sit up but then just leans back until his butt is on the ground and pulls his feet in front of himself.

"Sometimes, stupid things look like they might explode. But hey, at least I heroically saved you from garbage. That's a great story for your friends later." He shakes his head, staring at the bag that's quieted as the wind has died down.

"I would never do that. It's okay, Twiz. I don't get it, I can't, but it's okay."

"It's not."

He gets up and puts his hand out to me, pulling me to face him. His eyes are hard, a drastic change from just moments before when they were dancing.

"It's not okay, but it's not your issue either. I'm sorry I dragged you down with me. Literally."

This time I laugh, and he cracks the first genuine smile. I decide to drop it, for now, even though I want to make him share with me. We jog slowly the short distance to the parking lot.

"Twiz, it's not a big deal. If you were ready to start cool down and stretching, next time just use your words." I wink at him as I sit in the grass next to where we've parked, pulling one leg under the other. I purposely don't stare at him, but from the corner of my eye, I see him watch me as his breathing slows, not from the run we just finished but from whatever adrenalin just pumped through his system.

Eventually, he plops down unceremoniously next to me.

"Thanks. You know, for being cool about it."

"Don't mention it."

We finish stretching in silence while I ignore the hundreds of questions circling my head, begging to be asked.

Why does he teach self-defence for free? Why does he insist on only seeing a girl once? Why is he here with me now? What made him jump like that? What has he seen? What has he done?

How can I help?

Instead, I finish up and walk to Bethany.

"I usually stop for breakfast at the diner on the way home, if you're hungry."

He stops.

"Still want to hang out with me? Not worried you'll end up under the table next time I pass a garbage can?" He's joking but his eyes give him away again. He's scared.

It's a different look on him, one I can tell he doesn't know what to do with. I decide again to swallow the comfort I want to offer and let it go. I get the feeling he isn't interested in my sympathy.

"Just meet me at Humpty's."

5

TWIZ

*F*uck.

I have never reacted that badly to something like that before, so of course when I do, it must be around her. I didn't just knock her over, I jumped on top of her. I could have hurt her! All because I saw the bag and heard the crack of the plastic in the wind and expected an explosion instead of garbage like any sane person would.

I watch her shiny 'baby' pull out of the parking lot and sit for a minute to get my shit together.

Between the tongue biting tell I seem to have acquired and the garbage bag heroics, this whole return from war is not going as planned. This deployment was my fourth and while I've always taken time to get back in the swing of things at home, I've never had issues like this.

When I came back from Bosnia in 2000, while I was a little frustrated by the day-to-day parts of actual life, I didn't have any issue remembering where I was.

Then, there was my first to Afghanistan in 2005, and then the one in 2007 and even after what went down with Silas, I seemed to keep my head together better than most. I mean, sure, like everyone else, I had a few rough spots. It was harder than I thought it would be. But I was so focused on Tavish and Matt and the rest of the guys, I guess I never felt like it was more than I could handle. I mean, it's not like anything had happened to me, personally. I was just *there*.

I didn't regret any shot I had taken or the life it took. If anything, knowing I'd made some kind of difference made it okay.

This time, though, I can feel the shell cracking and I hate it. It's taken me too long after the shit storm when I was a kid to build those walls. They've served me well for too many years, at war and at home, and there's no way I'm letting them fall now.

I need to get a grip before things get worse.

I'm just not exactly sure how.

Once I'm breathing normally and can no longer feel every heartbeat in my chest, I head off towards Humpty's. When I walk in, I see Erika in a corner booth looking over a menu. She's pulled her damp hair out of the tiny ponytail and it's fallen into her face slightly, pieces stuck to the sweat on her forehead as her head is bent. Last time we were together, I was the one with the razor shaving all that gorgeous red off. The woman would look amazing in a mullet, but I must admit that hair is an improvement to the buzz cut I gave her. Her red-painted nail clicks on the side of her coffee cup, and I see her lips moving slightly as she reads, which for some reason I find adorable instead of dorky. I'd noticed it before, she's a tapper when she's nervous, which is common as far as tics go. She also tends to silently speak her thoughts, her lips moving slightly when she's analyzing something. It's almost imperceivable most of the time, but it's there. She's pulled a hoodie on over the sweaty top she ran in, but the zipper is down just enough that I can see the cooling lines that lead into her cleavage.

I stop there because these shorts won't hide anything.

She smiles at me when she sees me approaching and the way

her entire face lights up makes my heart still in my chest. An entirely different feeling from the pounding adrenaline earlier, it's more of a squeeze. I give my head the tiniest shake. That's not going to happen.

Instead, I sit and ask the waitress who followed me over for a coffee. She smiles at me a little too long before looking over and winking at Erika and finally heading off for the coffee pot. I look questioningly over but Erika just shrugs.

"Don't mind her. I come here every weekend, and I guess she's just surprised I have a friend with me." She waves off her hand like it's nothing, but I can tell by the way she won't meet my eyes, she's a little embarrassed.

Good, I don't like being the only one feeling off guard.

Erika pushes her menu to the side and grabs her mug with both hands like it holds the elixir to bring her back from the dead.

"I don't know why I look, I get the same thing every time." As soon as my menu is flipped, the nosey server comes back and takes our orders. I raise my eyebrows at Erika's order of the Canadian scrambler with bacon, toast, hash browns, and more coffee, but decide to order the same.

"Don't look at me like that. I just burned more than a thousand calories. This is one of the only times I can eat what I really want!"

I just shake my head at her and raise my hands in mock surrender.

"I didn't say a word!"

She narrows her eyes but doesn't respond. Instead, she points at my chest.

"Why do all your shirts look the same, and why are they almost pink?"

I glance down. I hadn't even noticed that I'd pulled a sweater on that basically matched the shirt I'd had on for the run.

"It's PT gear from work. PT is basically gym class, really, just for the Army. We all have to wear the same things, and every unit has their own. I have a ton of it, and it all looks the same. Regimental colours. And it's not pink, it's maroon. Aggressive salmon."

At this, she laughs aloud. "Are you serious? Dude, there's no shame here. It's pink."

"Aggressive. Salmon," I bite back, but there's no venom in my tone.

She's practically under the table, she's laughing so hard, and I can't help but chuckle a little too. It's not like it's the first time someone called it pink, and it won't be the last.

It's not pink, though, for the record.

"Whatever you say, Captain."

"Sergeant."

"Whatever."

"Not whatever!" I throw my head back in mock horror. "I'm not a captain. I'm not an officer at all. I'm a sergeant."

"Okay, okay. Man, who knew soldiers were so touchy. It's not pink and you're not an officer. Got it. Geez, you think guys who drive tanks and shoot things would be a little less emotional."

"Tanks? I don't drive a damn tank, woman!" When I look at her though, her eyes sparkle.

"You said that on purpose."

"I may have said something to Mark about tanks once, too. You guys are so easy."

I had forgotten her friendship with my old OC's wife. Being around her was so easy, how we met just seems to be a distant memory.

"You're killing me here."

The waitress comes over and leaves two massive plates of food in front of us before topping up our coffee. I hadn't realized how hungry I was until I could smell it and my stomach makes an embarrassingly loud rumble. Erika doesn't notice, she's too busy already eating.

We spend the next twenty minutes shoving our hungry faces with food without saying a word. It's not awkward, though, or weird. It's comfortable. Nice, even.

I'm not ready for this kind of normal with any girl, even if she's so far the most amazing one I've ever met. As soon as I'm done wolfing down my meal, I reach for my wallet, ready to make a quick break away from this woman who's getting far too close for comfort when she puts her hand over mine.

"You know, I barely remember the first time."

I know what she means right away, it's in the tone of her voice. I put my wallet down and turn towards her.

"I was that forgettable, hey?"

She smirks, "No, but we'd both had a lot to drink, makes everything a little fuzzy. I'm just saying it almost doesn't count, really, as a repeat if I don't even remember. I get it. You're not into commitments or whatever. I don't have time for that shit either, to be honest. But I do need a shower, and so do you. Seems like it would be a waste of water to not just hop into one together. And besides, you don't seem like the kind of guy who wants me to barely remember how good he was..."

Every part of my suspicious head screams for me to walk away. I don't do repeats for a reason. There're rules I must follow, for my own safety and hers. I can't afford to get attached to this woman, no matter how gorgeous or amazing or willing she is right now.

Somehow, though, through those screams, I hear my voice loud and clear as I answer her.

"Lead the way."

6

ERIKA

*W*e get to my apartment building and I pull into the parkade. I only have a few minutes to boot upstairs to my place and make sure there's nothing embarrassing on the floor of my bathroom before I hear him at the intercom. I buzz him up and then peek in my room, throwing a bra from where it hung in the shower into the laundry basket, and making sure the battery-operated boyfriend was safely away in the drawer and not on the nightstand in his bright-pink glory.

When I open the door for him, he's already there. "There were no spots in your visitor parking to fit the truck, so I had to park down the street," he says as he saunters inside. Just his presence in the small entranceway makes the room feel heavier, the air thicker. I want to run my fingers down the back of his arms where the muscle presses out from his sleeve. I shake my head. I don't know why I keep making such a big deal about this when I know it's just a hookup. I have more than enough experience with those, so there's no reason this should be any different.

Maybe because you've been daydreaming about this particular hookup for a year and a half.

I dismiss the thought and say the first thing that comes to mind.

"Why do you even have such a big truck, anyways?"

"No jokes about how my oversize vehicle must compensate for some part of my anatomy?"

I think I just actually blushed. "Nah, I never fell for all that. If I thought people used their vehicles to compensate for something, what would that say about me and Bethany? Besides, I've already seen your... assets, and you know well as I do, you have nothing to compensate for."

He breaks out into a shit-eating grin and makes a big production of adjusting himself in his shorts. It would be comical if my eye didn't linger far too long. I wasn't joking; he has nothing to be concerned about in that area.

"I guess, honestly, it's just the Saskatchewan boy in me. Town I grew up in, everyone had a truck. The bigger the better. I always pictured myself driving one when I was a kid. Can't say it's really needed here away from the farm life, but hey, I come in useful when someone has to move."

I think that might be the most he's ever divulged to me that's even remotely personal.

"Small town, hey? Where are you from?"

"Oh... nowhere you'd know. Really. It's tiny and boring. I left the minute I could enlist. This is a pretty swanky place you have here!"

He clearly changes the subject and I let him. We never signed up for anything more than superficial.

"Ya, I guess so."

I take a sweeping look around, trying to see with outsider's eyes what I've learned to take for granted. My building isn't far from downtown, but far enough that the neighbourhood is nice. I'm up high enough to have a decent view from the picture windows that fill a wall around my living room, with patio doors to the balcony. The room is superficially outfitted in leather couches and a decent-size TV on a dark-wood stand. I have generic art on the walls, a few family photos on the glass shelves that make up the half wall that separates that room from the kitchen. And with the marble countertops, cherry-wood cupboards, stainless-steel appliances, and generous-sized island in the center, I know that it stands out. I had chosen this place for its location and the natural light of the windows, but I try not to let myself forget the price tag it came with, or the fact that it would be way beyond most people's reach.

My gaze lingers on the kitchen table and my insides clench, remembering the last time he was here to see it. When I look up, there's the same hunger in his eyes, and we're both left staring without words between us.

We don't need them, however, because that table says enough.

I follow the same rules as he did to keep it from getting personal, and don't say anything more either. Not that this is what happens when you're an only child and you graduate university with no student loans because your guilt-ridden parents paid for it all, and that you moved right into a cushy job at the company owned by your dad, with a graduation present of a substantial down payment on a condo that most people couldn't afford even after years of work…

I work hard now. I earn what I make and then some. But having a place this nice at my age? That's nepotism and privilege at its finest. I get the feeling that might be a long way from his own experiences.

I glance back over at Twiz who has toed off his sneakers and is comfortably leaning against the island in my kitchen. He looks at home there, and the image makes me pause. Instead, I decide to take in the bulk of his shoulders and the way he's leaning to hide the bulge in his shorts.

My mouth gets dry suddenly, and I blurt something out just for the sake of making conversation.

"Where do you live these days?"

"Oh, Matt and I, he's another guy from work you would have met. He bought a place about a year ago and I rent half from him. It's just a bit farther north from here. We spent nearly 8 months of that in Afghanistan, and he's been gone home visiting family since we got back a few weeks ago. Can't say either of us hang out there much."

I think I remember him, the blonde who looks more like the college football star than a soldier.

"Is it nice? Having a roommate?" He cocks his head and I realize that's a strange question, but it's out there now and I can't take it back.

"I guess I've always had one. When I was a kid, once my little brother was born, I shared a room with him. Then when... well, after that I shared with another boy for a while at a different home. That was only a couple months though, then I left for the Army and I always had someone else with me. Sometimes, it's a ton of us in a tent, or it's just the guy in the shacks sharing the bathroom. I don't think I'd know how to live alone."

I want to go back to what he said about his family, and where he went from then, but I decide to just press forward so I don't pressure him. Besides, with the look that burns in his eyes, we won't be talking that long anyways.

"I was an only child. I lived in a big house where I could go all day without even seeing Mom or Dad. When they split, Mom's new place with... well, the place she lived after, it was the same. I stayed there through some of university, then back with Dad for a bit, and then I got this place. I don't know if I'm that good at sharing."

It doesn't escape me that we both just completely avoided entire topics in our answers. We make quite the pair. He seems lost in his head for a minute and the lust in his eyes clouds before he seems to blink it all away. When he looks over at me from where he's standing near the hall, his eyes tell a very specific story.

"What was that you said about a shower?"

With a grin, I walk while pulling my tank top over my head. By the time I pass him, I have everything off but my shorts. When I turn back around to look at him, I keep moving backwards towards the bathroom. He's not even trying to hide his excitement now.

"Well, let's go then, soldier. Teach me how to share the shower." I turn back towards the bathroom.

In a flash, he's right behind me, his breath on the back of my neck.

"Can do. For the record, though, this isn't how it usually works."

As I bend down to pull off my shorts from around my feet, I feel him pressed against me, and I can tell his shorts are gone, too, though I have no idea how someone can move that fast. I stay bent and turn on the spray of the shower, giving it a moment to warm. Turning as I stand, he has my face in his hands before I'm even all the way upright.

We fumble in, the shower curtain almost coming down around us a few times as we try to get over and into the tub without separating. As soon as we are situated under the spray, he hoists my legs up to his hips and presses my back to the cool wall, making it arch into him. At five foot nine, the ease that he keeps me balanced with one hand on my ass is sexy enough in itself.

"Shouldn't we use soap?" I ask breathlessly when his mouth finally leaves mine and moves down to my collarbone.

"After," Is all he says before he devours me again, his other hand moving between us, stroking me through the streams of water falling and pooling there. I feel my whole body clench as he pushes me higher and higher, his tongue mimicking the movements of his fingers in my mouth.

There's a shift and I feel him throbbing against me before he drops his head to my shoulders.

"Condom," he pants.

"I'm on the pill. And I've been checked since the last... I mean, I'm good if you are."

"You trust me?" This time he has his eyes on mine when he speaks.

"I had a medical before I went to Afghanistan, and I haven't been with anyone since I got back. And I've actually never done this without..."

My heart does a strange, happy little flip to hear him say he hasn't been with anyone when I know he's been home a few weeks now. I wasn't expecting that, Twiz is definitely a different girl every night type, I know because I'm one of them. And it's not an exclusive club. I can't dwell on why it makes me happy, because in one motion, he's inside me and my brain stops working completely.

His fingers go back to their perfect ministrations and before long, we are both gasping for air, spent, sweat mixing with the water from the shower as he slowly lets my feet back down to the floor.

"Well, I guess it's time for the soap now."

7

TWIZ

*E*verything about Saturday was off.

Starting with Friday night. What possessed me to head home early, without even finishing my drink, so I could go for a run with some girl, I'll never know. Not when I just got back from deployment and haven't even gotten laid yet. I don't even want to admit how hard keeping up with her was when I've just spent that many months with little time for exercise.

And for a girl I'd already slept with? I have strict rules and those aren't just for my own benefit, they're for everyone's safety. I have no choice, I can't let women in and I don't sleep with them more than once. Ever.

But she's gotten close. Too close. Starting with the fucking amazing way she looked in her running clothes, to the easy way we fell in step while we were out and ending with the mind-blowing sex in the shower, I'm far past where my rules have ever let me get before.

I hightailed it out of there once we were dried off, making some excuse about meeting friends. Which was entirely a lie. I spent the rest of the weekend bumming around my place, reminding myself why I could never do that again. I even cleaned up. Anything to distract me from wanting to see her.

I need to get a grip because I'm going to have to see her at least sometimes. She'll be at my class Friday. Picturing her in her workout gear, rolling on the mats with me in class is enough to set my mind wandering again.

I shake my head.

Absolutely not. That can never, ever happen again.

I pick Matt up from the airport today, and work starts again tomorrow. It's been a nice few weeks off, but I'm also ready for something to fill my days. That time off is probably nicer for people with families to spend time with.

After this many deployments, I've learned that as amazing as it sounds when I'm still there, the extended leave when we get home wears on me quick. It's just me and I tire of my own company fast. I wasn't lying when I said I didn't know if I'd know how to live alone, and I don't even have a damn dog because I don't know what I'd do with it when I'm gone. So, where that's usually left me is with an endless rotation of different women in and out of my bed, plenty of cheap whiskey, and work. Work took more of my life than was probably healthy, but it's been what's kept me sane these years. Take it away and I don't know what to do with myself.

I joined the infantry as soon as I could legally leave on my own. I knew I needed somewhere I could control the violence I was bred with, and it's become a part of who I am now.

I was hell on wheels for the first few years. I hadn't had any intention of enlisting up until the moment I did, and once I finished training, I was just so glad to get out of the shitty town we lived in, I didn't think about anything but my next party, my next drink, my next woman. I wasted more than a little time, a shit soldier just going through the motions, doing the bare minimum they required. Bosnia came and went without any real issue, but I was just a warm body on a late rotation where they figured I couldn't do too much damage. Constantly in trouble, marking time in the parade square, detained to barracks, skirting in late.

Then after 9/11, when the first deployment of guys left for Afghanistan and I wasn't on it because I was too drunk, too unreliable, holed up in some administrative platoon where they could keep an eye on me, I decided that shit had to change.

I worked my ass off. I was the guy volunteering for duty for a while, the guy willing to take the crap jobs. I deserved it all to earn the trust of my command back. I did, though, and soon managed to get onto a career course that would move me up. Things got so busy for the Army after that, with Afghanistan needing more and more soldiers, it was easy for me to have the opportunity to prove my worth.

By the time I was promoted to sergeant, just before we left on this last tour, even the sergeant major who gave me the rank was impressed.

Don't get me wrong, I kept up with the party.

I just kept the party out of work from then on out.

Lately, though, it's like I'm losing the drive. The middle of this last deployment, when I went on leave for two weeks, instead of hitting up Thailand or Amsterdam or all the regular haunts for single soldiers blowing off steam, I went to Germany and France, did a battlefield tour with Mike who met me out there. We spent the time bouncing from historical site to site during the days and pub to pub during the nights. We slept in hostels and cheap hotels. And I always slept alone. It wasn't even for lack of opportunity; the European backpacking community had more than its share of women willing for a quick encounter in a cheap room or even the bathroom of the bar. I just... didn't. I told myself at the time, it was because I had gone there with Mike and I didn't want to ditch him for an easy lay, but that was a lie.

I just wasn't interested.

This needs to change, because I have a lifetime ahead of me still and anything more than the quick, relationship-free sex and arms-length friendships with the guys is not in the cards for me.

When you come from stock like mine, you don't get to decide to settle down one day. I get my job, which can thankfully take up more than enough of my time, I get my truck, and sometimes, I get a willing woman in my bed.

She just can never stay there.

So, as much as I want to track Erika down again before the next class, to find myself back out at a restaurant with her, back in her condo, back in her shower... I can't.

I'm sitting in the pick-up lot at the airport when I see the familiar face ambling over, his green duffel slung over one shoulder, backpack on his back. I might be the one wooing a different girl in my bed each night, but Matt, he's the one with the looks for it. He looks like the definition of boy next door, short, blond hair, bright-blue eyes, a way about him that I imagine would be considered charming. If there was ever a guy that a girl would want to bring home to meet Mom and Dad, it would be him.

I have yet, however, seen him take advantage of it. And I live with the guy, so if anyone would, it would be me. No, Matt is a genuine, hundred-percent, good guy. Even with the trail of women who moon after him everywhere he goes. There was even a short time that I wondered if maybe he batted for the other team, since I had never seen him with a woman. I wouldn't care either way, to be honest, but that's not it, though. I've seen him flirt and it's always been with girls, I've even seen him go on a date or two. I'd like to think I know him well enough, and I'm observant enough, that I've seen who catches his eye, even if he never acts on it. I'm not sure if he's just really picky, or there's something more, but he just... Waits.

I don't even think he knows who he's waiting for, but he does anyways.

I hear the duffel bag hit the bed of the truck before the door opens and his backpack is thrown in before his body.

"Hey man, thanks for the ride."

I just grunt and pull away from the lot. He doesn't have to thank me, of course I picked him up.

"How was home?" He doesn't respond right away, and I take a quick glance at him while I pull out onto the highway.

I think he looks… worse than when he left. And that's saying something, because we had just finished almost eight months in the desert when I dropped him off.

"You know, same old whatever. Mom and Dad are still crazy. Food was good, it was a'right." His answer isn't an answer at all, but I don't push him.

I can't say that I think about how our friendship works, much, but I know it's different, especially within the military. He's an officer in my unit and I'm not, and people on the outside wonder all the time how we navigate that. Truth is, we just don't give it a lot of consideration. I met Matt back when he arrived as a brand-new second lieutenant to battalion. I was a master corporal just back from my second deployment, my first tour to Afghanistan. He is a few years younger than I and at that time, it seemed like a much bigger divide than our ranks. Though now, we don't much notice. We seemed to always be at the gym at the same time in the mornings and got to talking. Being that he was a lowest man on the totem pole officer and at first, not in my platoon, it never really mattered all that much that we became friends. We started running together, training for Mountain Man. By the time he was moved in to be our platoon commander for my next deployment, we were already tight. I'd guess lately, most of the younger guys at battalion wouldn't even necessarily know we're roommates. At work, we are professional, but for our friends, it's never much mattered.

Sometimes he gives me shit. Sometimes I pull out a 'with all due respect, sir…' but at home, we mostly just fight over dishes and who has to make the phone call to the pizza place.

We both hate the phone.

I think we get along best because neither of us is one to ask many questions. On drunk nights when I've probably said more than I should, he doesn't make me talk about it the next day. And on rides like this one, when I can tell he wants to let it go, I let him.

Matt knows more about me than anyone else.

That's still not a hell of a lot but shows how much I trust him.

Back at the house, we are both quiet. Tomorrow at work, we'll start the new positions we've been moved to. I'm moving to a platoon and Matt's moving into a more administrative role that I know he's dreading but just comes with his career progression. He's slated for big things, just like his general father before him.

I get the impression that's not Matt's greatest priority, but he can't change who he is, or his last name.

Well, you can change your last name, it only takes a few papers and a bit of cash to become a Sampson. I learned that twelve years ago. I could hide where I came from, though, because it's not right there in everyone's face.

For Matt, even if he did ditch the Christianson name, though, he'd still be the general's son. There's no getting out of that.

By seven that night, we're sitting on the floor of the living room with two separate piles of kit in front of us, sorting all the last-minute things from deployment to bring back to work with us. The History Channel is playing some random show on World War 2 and neither of us has said anything in an hour or more.

By the time we both call it a night, I can almost feel the

weight of what's on both our minds sitting in the room. Part of me even wishes one of us had it in us to say it aloud.

Instead, I hit his shoulder with mine as I head downstairs to my bedroom and he heads up to his.

"Good to have you back, man."

In the morning, I wake up far too early, with my head filled with everything I need to get done at work. When I head up the stairs, Matt's already gone, even though the sun is barely up. He is an early riser every day, but this is early even for him. Starting the new job must have really stressed him out. I grab a bowl and pour in the Lucky Charms, plopping it down in front of the TV where I turn on some news morning show while I eat.

I hardly hear any of it, it's not until I'm walking back to the kitchen that something catches my attention.

"Sad news out of Ontario today, as a thirty-five-year-old Canadian Forces veteran in Deep River has been found dead from an apparent self-inflicted gunshot wound in a wooded area near his home. Investigators then found the bodies of his twenty-seven-year-old common-law wife and her three-year-old daughter inside.

Police continue their investigation but say they are not looking for any more suspects. It appears to have been a murder-suicide..."

The ringing in my ears takes over and I don't hear the rest. I don't even hear the bowl hit the floor, or the front door opening.

All I see is the police tape.

"Son, you Robbie Portier?" And in my head, I'm running. Past the police, into the house where Sam is lying on the stained carpet, his tiny body twisted.

So much blood. So, so much blood.

"Son, you can't be in here." His body is so small. So small. I'm trying to pick him up but a weight from behind is stopping me.

"Where's my mom? Where's Steven?" My voice doesn't even sound like mine and later, they'd tell me they were first suspicious because my first question wasn't what happened or who did it.

And they'd be right. I already knew the answer to both those questions.

My eyes peel from Sam and that's when I see her arm in the doorway to the kitchen. She's crouched over something, hiding it beneath her, her body contorted, blood sprayed around her like someone dropped a can of red paint.

"Mom! Mom!"

There's another pressure on my arm. It's not from the cop behind me. I go to brush it off, but it holds on and I hear another strange voice that doesn't belong in this house.

"Hey, Twiz, that's my hand. That's my hand because I'm here, in front of you."

Matt? Matt shouldn't be here. I don't want him to see. I don't want him to know what I'm capable of.

"Twiz, can you look at me?"

I blink, and Sam's body disappears. So does the room. Matt's blue eyes stare into mine.

"That's it. Tell me five things you see right now."

I take a deep breath and look around.

"My kit. The cereal bowl. The coffee table. The couch. Your stupid face."

He chuckles.

"And four things you can touch."

I put my hands down from where they were fisted in front of me.

"The carpet. The milk on it. My feet." I wiggle my toes. Then I reach out and smack his leg. "You're stupid leg."

He doesn't respond that time, "Three things you can hear."

"The TV. The cars outside. Your stupid voice."

My breath is coming slower now, and I blink a few more times, getting my bearings.

"Two things you can smell."

"Milk. And you, you stink." He doesn't even smile.

"One thing you can taste."

I run my tongue along my teeth.

"Blood."

Matt takes a deep breath. "Okay, let's start over…"

"No." I stand up in front of him so he stands too.

"It's okay, Twiz. We have lots of time. We can just…"

"It's fine, Matt. That part was still real. I must have bit my tongue when I dropped." That's a lie, I didn't bite it. I was biting it. Over and over with my eye tooth. Like I've been doing without thinking since I got back. But he doesn't need to know that.

"Where did you come from? I thought you were at work already."

"Nah. I just couldn't get back to sleep this morning so I… went for a drive for coffee."

He immediately bites down on the inside of his bottom lip.

At least I'm not the only one with a tell. He's lying.

"So, want to tell me what that was about?" I don't. I really don't. If I play this right, he might just assume it's because of the deployment and let it go. I don't know if that's better, though, but at least I can talk about that.

I lean down, grabbing my bowl and spoon and taking them to the kitchen, flicking off the TV as I walk past.

"Want to tell me where you really were?"

He says nothing, and I finish cleaning the mess I had made in silence. When I'm done, I see him heading to his room to change as I head to mine.

"Matt? Where did you learn to do that?"

He looks at me sadly. "I knew someone once that would have a lot of panic attacks."

I'm struck with the realization that this is my best friend, and there's so much I don't know about him.

"I didn't have a panic attack. I'm not crazy. I just zoned out for a minute."

"Sure." He turns away and keeps walking.

"Matt? Thanks, hey?"

"Ya, man. Just... Talk to me one day, will ya?"

I don't answer. I don't want to make promises I can't keep.

Back in my room, I strip out of my sweatpants and pick up the combats that I washed and laid out last night. The green ones, a change from the desert tan I had been wearing for the last eight months. I find myself staring at the pattern, peeling and unpeeling the Velcro of my nametag on the shirt. They don't look right, like there's a piece missing but I'm sure there's not. I've been wearing the same ones since they changed over from the olive drab many years ago. Other than the slip on that shows my rank, they've always looked the same. My dog tags are tossed on the counter. I rarely have them on when I'm not overseas, and I haven't even looked at them since I first got back. I pick them up, letting the chain run down the tag in a rhythmic, metallic pull. I throw them in the pocket, hooking the chain through a belt loop, and then pull the pants on and put my arms through the sleeves of my shirt. I stare at the plain full-length mirror propped on the wall by the door to my room. It takes me awhile before I realize why they look wrong.

They're clean.

I shake my head as the image of the blood spatter and sand that I picture covering my uniform fills my mind. I close my eyes and take a deep breath before looking back in the mirror.

Still clean.

I wonder if that will ever look right again.

8

ERIKA

I'm still staring at the same computer screen that sucks my life when a loud buzz comes from my purse.

I barely use text messages even with friends, so the strange alert catches me off guard and I dig my phone out.

"Don't know why you keep trying to run from me, Bitch."

Ugh, I thought the last time I changed my number, I'd managed to at least limit his messages to my work email and snail mail. I hit delete and make a note to call and block that number. Not that it makes a difference, he just uses different ones.

When my mom left my dad for someone barely older than I was, I thought the rumours would be the biggest issue. Instead, I ended up with this. I thought after the shit show that went down when I was in college, it was over, and he'd leave me alone, but he never did. Once my mom decided she was done with him about five years into their pathetic marriage, it seemed to only get worse.

Don't get me wrong, it wasn't me coming to her in tears confessing what he did that made her leave him. No, nothing like that. It was just someone younger with more money. I'm not sure where he's even living now, or what he does, but he's always sure to send creepy flowers, harassing emails, and disturbing text messages every once in awhile just to keep me on my toes.

He's never actually spoken to me since then, though, so it's been easy to just get used to ignoring him. It used to keep me up at night but these days, after so long, I barely even think about it. I can control almost everything in my life. My weight, my work, my training. I don't have time for what I can't control.

"Who is it, sweetie?" I look up to see my dad standing in the doorway of my office, probably noticing the scowl I must have had on my face as I put my phone back in my purse. A quick glance behind me and I can see the others in the cubicles behind him all looking over. In a professional setting, you don't call your office manager sweetie.

Far be it from my dad to care, though.

"No one, Dad. What's up?"

"I thought maybe we could go for lunch? My treat. I feel like I never see you anymore..."

The man is the king of guilt trips. He just came over for brunch on Sunday, and it's only Friday. I was looking forward to maybe finishing up here a little early, so I could get a workout done at the gym before class.

That's not going to happen if I'm out for lunch with my dad.

"I guess I could really quickly..."

He doesn't even let me finish before he's grabbing my jacket for me from the rack beside the door and holding it out for me. I get up reluctantly.

"We're taking Bethany."

He just grunts, and we drive in silence to the small Vietnamese restaurant around the corner of the office, our go to. Once we are situated with our orders in, he finally speaks, "I spoke to your mother yesterday."

58

"That's nice."

I haven't spoken to my mom in years. Not since junior year at college when I finally broke down and told her what my 'stepdaddy' had been doing and she laughed in my face.

"She's getting remarried soon. She'd like to see you."

"Not going to happen."

My mom and I, we looked very much alike. Our red hair, green eyes, sharp features, slightly too big for our face lips. Like her, I struggled with my weight. Always carrying an extra fifty pounds or more almost since puberty, I was uncomfortable in my body. Mostly because my mom, who had basically the same figure, was constantly belittling herself. I'd hear her every day when I was growing up, complaining about how fat she was, how gross she looked. How she didn't know how Dad could even look at her. Then I'd look at myself and realize that if she was gross and fat, so was I. And it stuck. I didn't bother with makeup, didn't even try to find flattering clothes. I just hid under sweaters and leggings, alternating between starving myself during the days and stuffing my face at night. Too embarrassed to try to work out.

But then sometime in my early teens, my mom decided to start seeing a trainer. She had some surgery, went to the gym a ton, and counted every calorie. Until one day she was finally her definition of 'pretty.' Stick thin, with sunken cheekbones and augmented breasts, a tummy tuck and a fake tan. All paid for by my dad's hard work. Which he was fine with, as long as she was happy, until she up and left him as soon as the transformation was complete. Calling my dad fat and useless, I would listen late in the night when she'd admonish him for not being motivated like her to look his best. Until one day she finally told him she just wasn't attracted to him anymore. And off she went, moving in with her barely twenty-one-year-old personal trainer before the divorce papers were even finalized. With half my dad's money, she laughed at him even after she was gone.

The first years were bitter. Steve, my new 'dad,' was barely five years older than I, and to say my parents fought a lot at that time was an understatement. It was a war zone between the two of them. That's when Steve started to try to get to know me. He would tell me how he knew this must be hard and he just wanted to be a listening ear.

So, he'd pick me up from school, take me out to eat, talk to me about classes, friends, and everything else. He was so close to my age, he became more of a friend than any kind of laughable father figure. So, when my parents finally got along long enough to suggest that I move in with Mom during university, I agreed easily. I figured even though I was still mad at my mom, Steve at least would be there.

It wasn't until I was a seventeen-year-old, nervous for my first week of university, that he offered me a beer while Mom was out at a 'retreat.' One beer. Then several. Then he cornered me on the way to my room, telling me how pretty I was, how he'd always loved my curves. I can still remember laughing at him. My mom had so many times reminded me how much 'better' she did in life once she lost weight in her attempt to encourage me to do the same. There was no way he wanted me the way I looked. But he wore me down, small touches, compliments, until I believed him.

And I let it get too far.

Way, way too far.

So, when I ran home a year later, with my tail between my legs, and asked Dad if I could move back with him until school was over, I just told him that Mom and I weren't getting along. Which was true.

I just didn't tell him it was because I slept with her husband.

I certainly didn't tell him that when I came to her in tears, she didn't even have the decency to believe me, either.

Instead, I kept up in university, joined a running club, lost fifty pounds, and vowed that part of my journey would be to never, ever let myself be that chubby, naive girl again.

I take what I want on my terms and I fall for no one.

Which has never been a problem until I met a certain drop-dead gorgeous soldier who I can't get out of my head.

"I didn't think you'd want to see her, but I told her I'd let you know. I think the wedding is in August."

This will be her third marriage after my father. After her and Steve ended, she moved right on to John. That lasted even less time than Steve did.

I think this new guy's name is Carl.

I'm pretty sure he's my age. And since Mom is in her mid-fifties now, no matter how often I remind myself that age shouldn't matter, it doesn't make me want to meet him. Besides.

Third.

I can't be expected to keep caring.

"That's nice for her." I try my best smile as I tuck into my small bowl of pho, one of my favourites.

"That's nowhere near enough food, Erika."

As much as my dad has moved on from his feud with my mom, he's still unbelievably insecure. He hates my weight loss. I think in his head, it's just a sign that I'll leave him, too, just like Mom did after she lost weight. And even though he's reaching sixty and could really use some exercise for his own health, it's not even worth trying to bring that up, either. He sees it as a personal attack. After what my mom put him through, I don't blame him, but I want to see him move on with someone new. Be happy. Instead, he's stuck in this rut and I have no idea how to help him get out.

"Don't worry, Dad, once I'm done at the gym tonight, I'll have a nice, big dinner."

"You don't need to keep going to the gym. With the running, too, you must just tire yourself out. You're too skinny."

I stifle a sigh.

"I'm okay, Dad, I promise. What about you, what are your plans for tonight?"

"Oh, I don't know, honey, I'll just watch some TV and head to bed. I'm old, you know."

I just shake my head. We've had this conversation too many times that I know it's not worth trying anymore.

The bill finally arrives and I'm back at the office before one, finishing up and pretending I'm not unreasonably excited to see Twiz at class tonight.

I said it was just that one time. Just that one more go and I meant it. He hasn't called, and I didn't expect him to. I don't need him anymore than I need anyone else. Even if it was the best sex I've ever had.

The things that man can do with his hands… And the filth that comes out of his mouth? I'll hear that gravelly voice telling me what he wants in every fantasy I have for the rest of my life.

That doesn't mean I want to see him again.

When it's finally quitting time, I'm consciously trying to slow my walk down, to breathe normally, to stop thinking about him at all. I'm not a teenager, dammit! It's not working, and I make it from my desk to my car in record time.

My heart stops when I look at Bethany, though. There's a note on the dash that I notice exactly at the time as I feel the prickling on the back of my neck like I'm being watched. I spin around, my back to the driver's door, but I don't see anyone else in the underground lot. I reach back and grab the paper without even turning around.

"Told you not to run, whore."

It's written in black, permanent marker across a full-sized paper, the scratchy letters sloppy and uneven. I feel my vision tunnel and I take deep breaths, in and out like I have learned to do to keep the fear at bay. Using the keys I always have in my hand, I open the door, for the first time wishing I could do it with the push of a button like most new cars now. As soon as I slip inside, my bag pulled on my lap, I lock the doors and turn her over, putting her in drive and pulling out of the lot before I even have my belt on.

At this point, I just want to get to the gym. Get there and forget this. Which I realize isn't the best option when it comes to dealing with everything, but so far, the only way I've been coping. I remind myself of that extra drink I had this week, and the way I saw that little roll at the side of my bra. That's what I need to work on. The things I can control.

I'm scared, so I run. Literally.

When I get to the gym, I'm early again. I try to slow down, take my time changing so I'm not that girl who's always waiting in the room, so I don't give him the idea I'm trying to get alone time with him. Still, though, when I walk in the training area, I'm the first one there and I'm on the ground, one leg in front stretching when I hear the footsteps behind me and a hard body flops on the mat next to me.

"Hello, gorgeous."

My stomach doesn't do a happy little summersault at the sound of his voice. That would be pathetic.

"Hey there, Captain."

He just shakes his head.

"I'm not a captain. And I get enough sergeant at work. I'm no sir, either... how about master? I might get used to that, just from you though."

"Fat chance, soldier boy."

We finish stretching in silence and soon, the rest of the class walks in. Shane runs us through some Tabata, and I'm a hot and sweaty mess when Twiz pulls me up to demonstrate with him again.

"Today we're going to do some mat work. I'm going to have you and your partners simulate various situations where you might be pinned down, and we'll talk about the best options for defence from those positions."

Twiz loosely demonstrates some of the steps involved when using your hips to toss someone off you when they are on top, and each group finds their own spot on the mat to work on it. As usual, he spends the first few moments making sure everyone got the technique before coming back to me.

"All right, Hellcat, let's see what you've got." I lie on my back and he throws a leg over, sitting on my hips. I feel a hard ridge against my thigh and realize he's wearing a cup, which seems excessive, but I guess you can't be too prepared. After a few successful throws, he situates himself back up and then without warning, drops his chest against me, his forearms on my shoulders.

"You're a quick learner, so let's make this a bit harder..." He keeps talking but I can't hear him. All of a sudden, all I hear is the sound of the blood rushing in my head as I feel the heavy blanket of his hard body pressing me down on the mat.

"It will only hurt a minute, E. Just relax." I kick up my hips in jerking motions. It hurts. Oh God, it feels like my insides are tearing. I don't want to do this.

"Erika! Stop. Relax and let it happen." His breath in my ear smells like stale beer and the tears on my face pool in my ears. The way it makes them itch seems like an odd distraction from the burning between my legs...

"Stop! Steve, please, it hurts!"

All of a sudden, the pressure from my chest is gone and the rushing in my ears clears.

"Erika. Open your eyes and see me, Erika. It's me, Twiz."

I open my eyes and look around the room. It's silent, everyone in the room is watching me. The quick pants of my breath are the loudest noise. Twiz is up on his knees beside me, his hand out, hovering without touching. The pity in his eyes undoes me.

"Erika... I'm so..."

I'm out of the room before I hear him finish.

9

TWIZ

I'll kill him.

I don't know who he is or what exactly he did, but I will find him, and I'll make it hurt.

I changed immediately, having Shane watch to be sure she didn't leave without me, knowing it would have been faster if I didn't have to take the damn cup off. Erika and the rest of the class can think it's because I'm scared she'll take a shot at my boys. That's better than her realizing it's to hide my reaction to rolling around with her.

I stand outside the changeroom where Erika ran to, waiting. I considered running in after her, but thankfully my brain caught up with me and I realized running into the women's change room after a clearly traumatized woman, wasn't the best idea.

Besides, she probably needed time.

Twenty minutes later, I see her walk out and hold myself back from rushing at her. Her hair is wet from the shower, she's got jeans and a t-shirt on, no makeup, her bag slung over her arm. Her embarrassment is almost palpable, but she holds her head up. This girl is strong.

"Erika." I don't approach, just call her name from where I am on the far wall. She turns to see me, and I see her shoulders sink. If I didn't know it was because she clearly doesn't want to talk about what happened, and not because she doesn't want to see me, I'd almost be offended. She reluctantly heads towards me and I meet her halfway.

"Have time for a coffee?" I ask hesitantly. I think back to my conversation with Matt this week and I get that trying to get her to open up is completely hypocritical of me, but I have to try. For a moment, I almost wish Matt was here. He'd be much better at this.

"Any chance we can make it something stronger?" She gives a sad grin and I nod.

"Of course. I'll follow you to your place and you can ditch the car. Ride with me to the pub. If that's okay?" The soldier in me wants to take control of this, but I also don't want to make it worse for her.

She just nods, and we head to the parking lot. Once she's dropped her car, I drive in silence to the pub. I'm grateful it's still early. It isn't too busy, and I grab a booth in the back for us while she heads to the bathroom. I don't question her need to go again when we just left the gym. She still won't look me in the eye and far be it from me to tell her to stop stalling.

It's not too long before Juliette comes bouncing over, a smirk on her face.

"Was that Megan's friend? Erika?" She stage-whispers it, almost conspiratorially, like if someone hears her it might stop being true.

"Yup."

"Are you on a *date?*" I want so badly to play this off and say no, but I don't want to draw any more attention to Erika than she needs right now, and a date might get us a little privacy. Jules is right to be surprised, though. I doubt she's seen me on a real date even once in the time she's known me. Truth is, I don't know that I've ever been on one.

"Stranger things have happened, Jules. Pretty sure she drank whiskey and Coke with me last time, so grab two of those. Hers is a diet. I remember last time that was important. Then, just give us some date room, hey?"

Jules stands for a minute, opening and closing her mouth a few times, before she smiles and nods, skirting away only to come back with two drinks just as Erika walks back.

"Hey, Erika!" Jules just smiles in her direction and then winks at me, saying nothing else before she disappears.

Have to give her credit for trying, right? She was *almost* smooth.

Erika sits and takes a long sip of her drink before she says a word.

"I know I owe you an explanation..."

"You don't owe me anything. Ever. If you want to tell me what happened, though, I'm here."

She nods, and we are quiet for a minute. I glance over and see Jules pretending not to watch us as she wipes the same spot on the bar again. If she thinks it's a date, she must assume it's going badly.

"I'm sure most girls in the class have the same story, it's not exciting. I trusted a guy once, when I was preparing to start university. He convinced me he cared. And then... well, it turns out he didn't."

My blood is boiling, and it takes more effort than it should to keep my voice even.

"Was he charged?"

She sighs. "No. No, it wasn't... I mean, it started out consensual, and I don't think that could have happened. Even my own mother didn't believe me, really. It's not a big deal, anyways. It's been so long, and I mean, if I hadn't got the notes from him today, I'm sure I wouldn't have even..."

This time I don't have time to control my voice.

"What notes, Erika?" There's a harshness in my tone I wish wasn't there, especially when she flinches just a tiny bit. "I'm sorry. That came out wrong."

"It's okay." She takes a deep breath. "I just know you're going to think it's a bigger deal than it is. He just sends me texts every once in a while, sometimes flowers or notes. Just stuff like that. I've never actually seen him since though."

Something doesn't add up. If it was her first year of college...

"I thought you were older..." I mumble almost to myself and she gives a humourless laugh.

"Worried you've slept with a co-ed? I graduated college almost six years ago, Twiz, I'm twenty-seven."

"So, he hurt you a decade ago, Erika. You're telling me he's been doing this for a decade and you've never said anything?"

This time she doesn't flinch, she just gets mad. "There's nothing to say, Twiz. He doesn't come see me. Doesn't threaten me, just annoys me. Calls me names. Stuff like that. But he doesn't come to my work, or tell me he'll kill me, or anything bad. There's nothing the cops can do. It's okay. It's fine. *I have it under control.*"

"He doesn't really hurt me, Robbie. Don't make it a big deal. I'm okay." I shake my mom's voice out of my head.

"It's not okay! Stalking *is* really bad, Erika."

"Well, I'm no expert, but so's hiding from garbage bags, *Twiz.*"

I take a deep breath. She's not wrong, even if she's clearly just deflecting. "You're right. I don't have any right to tell you what to do, Erika. I just don't want to see you get hurt." *Again,* I want to add, but I don't.

So far, it feels like whatever this is between Erika and me is just as much about what we're not saying as it is about what we are.

"I won't. Honestly, it's been going on so long, it's fine.

Nothing ever happens. One of these days, he'll finally get bored of me and move on."

I want to say no. I want to tell her guys like him don't just move on. They keep pushing and it only ever gets worse. So much worse. I can't dwell on that, though, and I'm scared where my head will end up if I keep pushing her down that road. If I have to tell her *how* I know. Instead, I take a long drink. Every single instinct in me wants to demand that she come home with me and let me protect her.

Only trouble is, there would be no one there to protect her from me.

We drink in comfortable silence for a while. Jules eventually comes over with a menu, so we can order some dinner, and slowly, our early evening drink becomes dinner, and when Matt and Tav show up, I motion for them to join us and it moves to after-dinner drinks. Hours later, I'm still nursing my second drink, since I drove Erika here, but watching the boys get rowdy when I'm sober is a new experience, especially when I'm used to being the rowdiest of the bunch.

Jason and Beth are the last through the door, and I look at him for the first time in a while. It's warm out these days and he has shorts on, his mechanical-looking prosthetic displays below his left knee. Without seeing it, though, you couldn't tell he had it anymore. The crutch he had, and then the limp when he ditched the crutch, is virtually gone until the end of the night when it starts to get sore. His thigh muscles strain under the shorts and I swear his biceps might be as big as my head. He's always been a big guy, not necessarily the best trait for a tanker, but these days he's taken it to a whole new level. He's determined to convince the Canadian Forces he can stay in the military, even though it's never happened before. It's both stubborn and inspiring.

The red rim to his eyes, though, and his perpetually blown-out pupils are a different story.

I only have time to deal with one clusterfuck at a time, though, so I've been trusting that Beth has that shit under control for now.

Jules comes over to sit with us a few times once it quiets down after the dinner rush. There're only a couple of other tables left, and she divides her time between them and Tavish. That's when I realize Jeremy isn't here.

"Hey Jules, where's Jeremy?" She grins from where she's sitting on Tavish's lap.

"He has the day off, because he can. He's decided to be more of a real owner now that he promoted his bar manager to general manager." Tavish gives her a squeeze and this time I grin.

"No shit! Good for you, Jules! That's awesome!"

"Thanks! It's nice to put the school stuff to good use, and it means eventually I can schedule myself more daytime hours, so I have more time off with Slick when he's home. So, I'm happy. It also makes me a full-time employee, with benefits, which might just come in handy one day." She offers her husband a small smile, and I don't doubt there won't be too much time left before there's another announcement from those two.

I feel a little squeeze and swallow it down. I've never envied the people I know who have settled down before. I just can't, and there's no sense in wanting something you can't have. I like my bachelor life, my job. I don't need a woman for more than a night, and there's no way I could want kids, either.

It's no longer even an option, I took care of that almost a decade ago.

But fuck, if watching Jules smile at Tavish doesn't make something hurt knowing I'll never have what he does.

I look over at Erika. The pale skin of her chest visible just above her shirt is flushed, and she's talking animatedly with her hands to Jason about some obstacle race she did a couple of years ago. She's had a few drinks and she looks relaxed, almost soft. It's not her usual look, but it's a good one on her. The curve of her collarbone to the small silver chain around her neck, the crease at her eyes when she smiles, all these things I've never once even noticed in another woman are all I can't help seeing on her. I catch myself smiling like a dork as I watch her, and Matt elbows me.

"She's good for you," he says with finality.

"I'm not good for her, man. You know I don't do repeats."

He opens his mouth as though he's going to say something, but he doesn't. Just shakes his head. My eyes flick back to her and this time she catches them with hers. I can tell she's ready to go.

"All right, runner. I better get you back in time for that early morning you have."

She nods and says goodbye to the group before I follow her out to my truck. The drive to her place is quiet but not uncomfortable. When I pull up in the visitor parking, she looks over to me as I park.

"I'll be walking you upstairs, Hellcat."

"I can get myself to my condo just fine, Twiz."

"You can. But I'm going to walk you."

She shrugs and hops out of the truck, and she lets us in the front door of her building. Her apartment is on the tenth floor, but I'm not surprised when she goes to the stairs and we head up.

"I need to at least attempt to work off some of that alcohol." She smiles sadly.

"You ever let yourself off the hook?"

"No," she says with confidence and no room for argument.

Well then.

When we get to her floor, I'm probably a little too happy that at least I'm not the only one a little out of breath. I stand beside her while she digs in her purse for her keys and unlocks her door.

71

"Good night, Erika."

She looks at me strangely, probably expecting that I would have tried to get her to invite me in. Every part of me screamed the same thing, but I don't. She gives me a soft smile before shutting the door, and I lean against it, waiting for the sound of her deadbolt.

It's far too long after I hear it lock while I rest with my back against her door, before I head back down the stairs.

10

ERIKA

I need to get that boy out of my head.

Last night, when I locked the door, I just stood there, leaning my forehead against it for way too long, stopping myself from the embarrassment that would come if I were to open it and call down to him, inviting him in again.

He's made more than clear that we've already used up any chances for repeats, regardless of how this weird friendship has developed. So, instead, I just stood there. Until several minutes later, I could have sworn I heard the sound of someone moving on the other side of the thin door, and then *I know* I heard footsteps walking down the hall.

It was probably a neighbour, but for the rest of the night, I tossed and turned, picturing what it meant if it was him. Was he fighting me as much as I was fighting him? Could I have convinced him for more? Do I even want to?

The little sleep that all those questions afforded did not make for an easy wake up at five forty-five this morning.

I pull into the parking lot at the trail a little later than usual, mentally chastising myself for another late night. I'm distracted when I get out, having to open the door three more times to put things back or take things out I've forgotten. It's usually a routine, I do it all the time, and yet I can't seem to get it together this time.

I click on the belt with my water bottle and turn around when something at the other end of the parking lot catches my eye.

A giant silver truck.

Leaning against the tailgate, watching me with a grin on his face, is the object of my entire frustrating night's desires. When he sees me notice him, he walks over.

Walking is not the right word. He saunters over, with the same infuriatingly confident swagger he always has, the grin only growing as he approaches.

"Good morning, Hellcat. I was starting to think you might not show." It takes me a moment to stop gawking at him before I come up with the right words.

"Well, I guess I didn't know there was anyone waiting for me."

Twiz leans down to tie his truck key to a shoelace, not coming across even a little bit concerned with my response.

"Turns out I enjoy these runs. And I could use the exercise after the months of nothing but heat and walking. So, I'm ready when you are."

I shake my head in a frustrated huff that I don't mean. I'm glad he's here. I'm always glad he's around. I'm far, far too happy to see him every time I do, and that's the biggest problem.

We make it to the opening of the trail and I break into a jog, with Twiz keeping pace beside me. Usually running with a partner is awkward, trying to find a middle pace that can accommodate both runners since everyone has their own. Twiz, though, seems an expert at just matching mine without needing me to adjust anything. He never pushes ahead, though I'm sure he could go out faster. He just keeps himself next to me regardless of my pace.

It's unnerving, like having a two-hundred-pound shadow. A crazy, good-looking, two-hundred-pound shadow.

The first few kilometers are run in silence. I had brought my headphones since I thought I'd be alone, but I don't turn them on. The sound of our feet on the trail and the intermittent noise of the city when it's close enough are the only things breaking the quiet.

"You didn't have to come just to look after me." I'm worried that after our talk yesterday, he thinks he needs to do this. I don't need a running partner that's only here out of obligation.

I don't need a running partner at all.

Twiz barks out a laugh.

"I don't do things I don't want to unless the Army tells me to. I told you, Hellcat, I just enjoy the run. So, as long as you don't mind the company..."

"I don't," I spit out, probably a little too fast.

We slip back into silence. Eventually, we pass the Port-O-Potties that were our turn-around point last time.

"So... I guess I should have maybe asked how far we are going?"

"Why, you getting tired there, Captain?"

He shakes his head.

"Not even a little bit. And for the record, if I really was a captain, I probably would be."

"Good. It's twenty-five today."

I think I hear the tiniest groan come from him at that statement and smile. Twenty-five kilometers should hurt at least a little; it's nice to see he's not superman.

"Well, this is one way to get back in shape."

It's a few more kilometers into the trail before it's time to turn around, and I stop at a bench for a moment to stretch. He plops on the grass next to me, pulling his leg under him and leaning back.

"You went back to work this week?" I decide to try to make at least a little conversation.

"Yup." His back sits straighter and his answer doesn't leave a lot in the way of follow-up.

"How's that going?"

"It's work."

He bites his tongue with his eyetooth after he answers, his eyes on the foot in front of him.

"You know, I get that I don't know much about any of this, but if you ever want to tell me about any of it. Or anything, you know..."

He lets out a long breath and lets his chest lean forward until it's almost touching his leg.

Holy crap he's flexible. His breathing is slow and deliberate, as though he's counting each breath, and watching the muscles in his back bunch and contract with each movement is more than a little distracting.

"It's... taking longer than usual for me to get my shit together, that's all."

I give a moment before I respond, seeing if he has more to add.

"That little... moment I had last week? It's happened a few more times. Maybe... more than a few."

Now, I sit next to him, mimicking his stretching position.

"That seems understandable, Twiz, I'm sure everyone..."

"I'm not everyone, though! This has never happened to me before and it can't! My job is everything!" he says that last part with what I'm sure is more desperation than he intended, and it squeezes my heart. I'm quiet a long time.

"I don't think there's a right thing for me to say here, Twiz, except that if you want to just talk through things, you know, about your deployments or anything, you can always do it with me. Consider it a running bubble. What's said on a run stays on a run."

He gives me a sad smile and jumps up, putting his arm out and pulling me beside him. We start off again, back the way we came, and I'm sure that's the last I'll hear of it. It was a dumb offer, and I should have known someone as closed off as him wouldn't accept it. Especially coming from me, when I don't know anything about the Army, deployments, or war. I let my mind drift as we continue along in silence.

Twenty minutes in, his voice almost surprises me. I think it might surprise him, too.

"The first deployment I didn't have any trouble at all..."

11

TWIZ

$\mathcal{B}$y the time I can see the parking lot in the distance, I can't believe the things that have come out of my mouth. I didn't get very far, mostly talking just about the places I've been and some of the things I've experienced. Still, far more than I ever thought I'd hear myself tell another person.

Nothing about the girl, though, or the way her body jerked when I hit her exactly where I was aiming, leaving no room for error. Or life.

I haven't gotten there yet.

I probably never will.

But it was a start.

I even told her about Silas.

"So, you guys knew there was always a rocket attack around that time at the camp, and you still tied that person to the bed?" Erika is horrified, but she's also laughing.

"We sure did!" I laugh along with her. I know it sounds bad, but it really wasn't.

Well, maybe it was, but also funny.

I don't know why I opened my mouth, why I've told her more about my time overseas in the hour we've been running than I've told anyone else in my whole career. Maybe she's just easy to talk to, or I'm just so tired of running, I'll do anything to keep my mind off it.

I know the truth, though.

It's that I really, really like this girl.

Dammit.

That shuts me up quick.

My legs are screaming by the time we make it back to the car, though I try my hardest not to show it. This woman is a machine. When we finally get to my truck and I throw my foot on the bumper, it takes effort to physically hold in the grunt at the tight stretch.

Erika's foot lands next to mine and I can't help but allow my gaze to trail all the way up her sweat-glistening leg. They're thin, but muscled, not at all skinny, just clearly athletic. Toned, with firm calves and thighs covered only marginally by the tiny running shorts she wears. Up close to her hip, I can see just the faintest stretch marks visible where her tan line is exposed as her shorts ride up. I've never noticed those before, but to be fair, when that part of her shows, I'm usually more than distracted. She doesn't have any children that I know of, so I momentarily wonder what caused them. Only for a moment, though, because I continue my perusal up, where there's a strip of skin showing under her tank top as she has one elbow up over her head, pulling her hand down. The position doesn't just expose her gorgeous strip of belly but makes her tits look amazing, pulled up and pressing against the top edge of her tank, and I stare unashamed, even when she catches my eye.

"I'm a sweaty mess," she says, looking away with just the smallest bit of pink on her cheeks that only makes her hotter.

"That's the way I like you," I answer without thinking. I quickly take my foot down, moving to the other side of the truck to continue stretching, but mostly to get my shit together. What the hell is wrong with me?

This is getting too close.

Erika strolls around beside me and I look over. The sweat pools into her cleavage, her damp hair is matted to her face, immediately reminding me of how she looks freshly fucked and splayed out on her bed.

I shimmy in what I hope looks like a shakeout from my stretch and not like an attempt to re-adjust the bulge in my shorts, but I know she's not fooled. Her smirk only makes her look sexier.

Damn.

Somehow, we end up back at Humpty's. I could swear that greasy eggs and hash browns have never tasted so good, after however damn many calories I just burned. We are quiet again, as I think back to all I shared with her. I can only imagine what she thinks of me. I talked her damn ear off like a teenage girl.

I blame that last drop of sweat that I watched nestle itself right between her breasts while she finished her coffee for my truck ending up outside her building again, my hand raised to knock on the door to her apartment.

When she answers, she looks as surprised as I feel at the fact I'm here. I don't want to talk about it. Instead, I just cover her mouth with mine, using my foot to close the door behind me.

I'm done talking.

12

ERIKA

*S*aturday mornings have become the highlight of my week.

Twiz is much gentler with me at class on Friday evenings now, much to my annoyance, but after spending all the time convincing me I could show my face again, he's been a total gentleman. With the addition of another class member several weeks ago, a tiny little thing named Jordyn whose mass of curly pink hair is almost half her height, he doesn't even have me for a partner anymore, which is probably for the best. Jordyn is much less likely to send me to the crazy place. I think she weighs the same as my dad's cat.

Sometimes after class, Twiz will meet me at the door to the locker room and we'll go for drinks or dinner. He always walks me back to my condo, no matter what, though, even if he has yet to come in those times. I know he thinks about it. I listen with my head on the door every night. It's getting longer and longer before he walks away.

But Saturday mornings? Even last week's thirty-six kilometers seemed to go by far quicker than usual. I want to say it's because a running partner makes everything go easier, but I know it's him.

He makes everything easier.

He's there, every week, no matter how early I make it or how late we were out the night before, leaning against his truck when I pull in. I enjoy watching him swagger over to me when I get out of the vehicle almost as much as I enjoy watching the muscles in his back move when he stretches.

Damn, this boy has me all messed up and I should hate it, but I can't.

Not when we spend our hours running the way we do.

He talks when we run.

He tells me stories of his deployments. His time in Bosnia. How terribly helpless it felt. The guys he's served with then and since.

The first few times, I thought it was strange he never talked about his family. Then I realize he does; his family just isn't the people he grew up with.

He tells me about Afghanistan. It started with just the funny stories, tales of the heat and the bugs and the pranks they pulled on each other. It eventually shifted, though. One day, he told me more about his friend Silas and it just slowly became the story of how he died. Of how Twiz watched his best friend hold Tavish back after the explosion, knowing they couldn't do anything to save him. About the mission after, when Tavish was already at home for the funeral and the rest of them went out and found the ones responsible.

There's no remorse in the story. You can see it in his face, hear it in his tone. He doesn't regret what they did, and he shouldn't. He doesn't give details, but when he assures me they paid for what they did, I believe him. It's not worth analyzing why I'm one-hundred-percent okay with it, either. More than that, I'm happy to hear it. Why shouldn't I be?

No, his remorse comes from the stories of afterwards. When

he tells how hard it was watching Tavish and Matt hurting, his voice is broken. He blames himself for not saying something earlier, not doing more. And though it clearly turned out okay for Tavish, he admits he wishes he had been the one to hold Tavish back so the guilt wouldn't eat at Matt.

He looks over at me surprised when he says that, as though he shocked himself with his words. As though maybe he's never considered himself a nice enough person to feel that way, to protect his friends that way.

He is so much more than he thinks he is.

Tonight is the final self-defence class. He's asked me if I'll demonstrate with him, showing off all that we've learned and then everyone can ask questions and practice what they're still unsure of. Twiz and Shane will go to each woman and give them the chance to practice on them, and he asked if I'd observe them as they do, in case he misses any cues that one of the women is starting to panic.

It's thoughtful of him, and something he's clearly spent a lot of time thinking on. Despite all he's shared on our runs, I can't figure out why he does this, but it means a lot to him and I'm happy to help.

I get into the gym and change, heading out to the mats just a little early, like always. I stopped feeling self-conscious about it, it's our routine now. Twiz stands inside with Shane, pointing at different corners, mapping out how the class will look. When he looks up at me, he smiles, big enough that his eyes shine. It takes me off guard, and my heart stuttering in my chest. He's stunning, his eyes managing to sparkle two colours at once, his teeth gleaming, his dark hair that seems able to look both perfectly put together and at the same time disheveled. He's always gorgeous without trying, but the way his face lights up just looking at me is enough to take my breath away.

It hurts almost as much, too. I'm sure he doesn't know what he's doing when he looks at me like that. If he did, he'd stop.

"Hey, Hellcat. C'mere, I'll show you the plan for tonight."

Shane gives me a quick hello, and we run through their plan. It all goes by in a blur once the others arrive. Twiz is shockingly gentle with each woman, asking permission before every movement. He doesn't touch anyone, even on the arm or shoulder, without asking first. Once he's sure they're ready, however, he really goes for it. He doesn't go easy on them, while I'm sure he doesn't use all his strength. He also doesn't let up. I watch each closely, but I didn't really need to. He seems to instinctively know when he's done, and he needs to back off. He always lets them finish with a sense of victory, but he's also sure they know it's not foolproof.

This isn't some volunteer gig he was roped into by a friend. This is personal. I just wish I knew why.

We come across Jordyn at the end. She's visibly nervous, chewing on a knuckle, her wild hair framing her face like a fuzzy pink silhouette. Twiz approaches her slowly, almost cautiously, and she attempts this weird half smile.

"Hey!" Her voice sounds forced and stilted.

"Hey, Jordyn! You're last up. There's a couple of holds that we can try to see where you're at with your training. I'll be the 'attacker' in this scenario, and I'm going to do my best to be as realistic as I can. I won't hurt you, but I won't make this easy, either. Are you okay with that?"

Twiz hasn't touched her yet, but Jordyn seems as though she's flinching from his very presence.

"Yes. Okay." Her voice is barely audible and I'm about to tell Twiz maybe we can skip this with her, but he approaches. He didn't lie, he's not going easy. He immediately lunges at her, and I can see he's attempting to take her back.

Panic flashes on Jordyn's face and it terrifies me. She's so tiny, with Twiz grabbing at her, she looks even more so. As fast as the panic appears, though, it's gone. She sets her jaw and then pivots, grabbing the back of his bicep like she was taught and spinning until she can push herself away. When he continues to advance, her hands are up, and she uses his one reaching arm as leverage. When he steps forward, she brings up a knee and before I know it, Twiz is dropped, his hands between his legs and a low, pained moan from his lips.

"Oh. Oh, oh, oh, I'm so sorry!" The panic is back on Jordyn's face and she covers it with her hands. I can still hear her muffled apology as I see tears spring in her eyes.

Twiz is off the floor quickly, though I can tell not easily. I can see his throat working as he swallows repeatedly, catching his breath. He reaches to Jordyn but still doesn't touch her.

"No, no, you have nothing to be sorry about. baby girl, that was amazing. You got me good. That was perfect!" His eyes water as he stands with his hands on his knees, but he's got a half smile on his face, and it's easy to tell he's proud. He's just also in a hell of a lot of pain.

Shane jogs over with an ice pack. "Holy shit, Jordyn, you're awesome! We haven't had someone take him down like that in forever! Great job!" Shane laughs, and Twiz gives him a look that could kill before smiling back at Jordyn.

"Awesome job, baby girl. Really. I'm not mad. I'm proud! I'm... I'm just gonna go sit a minute and nurse my wounds..."

Jordyn looks like she doesn't know what to do. Her eyes dart between Shane and Twiz and the rest of the class. I see it coming before she bolts, and I give a quick nod to Twiz before I head after her into the changeroom.

"Hey, Jordyn." She's in one of the stalls, so I sit on the floor, my back to the closed door. There's no one else in here, thankfully, with the after-work rush gone home.

The echo of the open space carries my voice.

"Hey." She sniffles.

"You didn't do anything wrong, sweetie."

I hear her soft crying for a moment before she answers, "I didn't mean to hurt him."

"He'll be okay, Jordyn. Hazard of the job. Plus, I know he was wearing a cup, so it wasn't too bad. Probably just take him a second. You know how overly sensitive men are about their balls. You'd think they were made of glass."

She gives a soft chuckle and we sit there for a moment after in silence.

"You probably think I'm crazy."

I laugh. "Jordyn, before you joined the class, one Friday I freaked out so bad when Twiz was on top of me, I screamed hysterically in front of everyone and ran away."

"Really?" Her voice sounds so small and I remind myself that I'm pretty sure she's close to a decade my junior, which would put her barely out of her teens, if that. My heart breaks for whatever brought her here. I won't ask, though. Especially not here on the floor of the bathroom.

"Really."

She's quiet for a moment. "I wasn't always like this." I'm trying to think of a response to that when she continues, "I used to be fearless. I used to get mad at myself for being too loud. I was always talking too fast, always the center of the party. I remember when I would actually try to be quieter..." She gives a humourless laugh. "Now, I can't remember the last time I went anywhere or talked to anyone I didn't have to. It takes work just to get every single word out."

"We all cope with trauma in different ways, Jordyn. Sometimes, we try to make ourselves bigger. Sometimes, we try to make ourselves smaller. There's no right way to grieve what was taken from you."

"I feel like... I feel like they took *me* from me."

My heart stops at the word *they*.

Jesus.

"Jordyn, are you safe now?"

"I'll never be safe."

I freeze. My mouth opens, trying to think of what to say

when I see Twiz's shape in the doorway. His hands are fisted at his side.

He heard her.

He's gone as fast as he arrived, and I blink before turning my attention back to Jordyn.

"Is there anything I can do?"

She gives that same lifeless laugh. "No, no. I'm sorry. I didn't mean to bug you..." I can hear her moving around now, probably standing up from the lid of the toilet. I stand too, my tired legs screaming at me as I unfold them from under me on the tile floor.

"Jordyn, you're not bugging me. At all. Are you busy tonight? Maybe we could have coffee?"

The door opens in front of me and she takes me in, her eyes red but dry now. Her hair almost an entity to itself, dwarfing her frame.

"Are you sure? You don't have to. I mean, your boyfriend probably wants..."

"Jordyn, I don't have a boyfriend." She just looks at me for a moment and gives the first real smile I think I've seen.

"Does our teacher know that?"

I'm left standing with my mouth open while she heads to the sink to splash some water on her face and run some through her hair, taming it just a little.

"Twiz is just a friend."

"Sure. Well, I'd like to have coffee with you. So, I should warn you. I tend to be *friends* with girls *and* guys. That's not the kind of friend I was hoping we'd be, though. No offence."

I laugh because I think I just caught a glimpse of the old Jordyn.

"I'm too old for you, I'm afraid. So, let's just be regular friends, okay?" I put my hand out and she hesitates only a moment before she takes it in hers and lets me give it a squeeze.

"Let me take a shower, okay?" I quickly strip and jump into

one of the stalls, rinsing off the sweat from the class. I throw on some jeans and a tank top, pulling my still a little too short hair up into a messy almost bun. It's been over a year since I shaved it with Megan, but I will be so happy when it's long enough for a decent ponytail again. I run some lotion over my face and slap on some mascara. I can still hear Jordyn in the shower so I zip my bag quick and step out so I can have a moment to talk to Twiz.

As I expected, he's leaning against the wall next to the doorway when I walk out.

"How's the boys?" I ask, gesturing to his crotch. He grimaces.

"They've been better. Happy to let you look and nurse them back to health, though..." He smiles, then seems to remember himself.

"Is she okay?"

"She will be." I give him a small smile. The concern on his face isn't forced, he is genuinely worried about her. I love that about him.

Dammit, now is not the time to analyze what that thought meant.

"I'm sorry. I knew no one else was in there so I just wanted to make sure she was okay. I didn't mean to hear... *Fuck*, Erika, she didn't say he. She said *they*! She said she's not safe!"

I glance behind me as I hear the shower shut off. I lower my voice.

"I know. I know! I don't know how to help her, Twiz... We're going for coffee and a chat." He nods.

"Oh, and Jordyn thought you were my boyfriend," I say it as a joke, but I watch his face shudder, so I immediately backtrack. "Don't worry, I set her straight."

He's quiet for a minute.

"Okay."

I thought for sure he would have a smartass comment for that, but he says nothing else. A moment later, Jordyn appears from the change room. Her face clean and fresh with no makeup in sight, and her bright pink hair still damp. It lies so much closer to her face and makes her look even smaller without its extra shape. She's wearing a hoodie, even though it's almost twenty degrees out, and a baggy pair of jeans with worn sneakers. She holds back when she catches a glimpse of Twiz.

"Hey, baby girl. Great job today, yeah? I haven't had a student drop me like that in forever. Amazing. You've learned a ton!" Her shoulders drop back down a little and she stops her retreat.

"I'm sorry you got hurt," she almost whispers.

"I'm not." Twiz shakes his head. "I teach this class a few times a year. I'd love for you to come back next time!"

"Really?" She uses that same voice that reminds me how young she is. With her makeup washed off and her hair controlled, her body covered in the oversized sweater, she looks like a child.

"Of course! Anytime." Twiz hands her a piece of paper.

"This is my number. Please call me if you ever need something, okay? If you are scared or you get hurt somewhere, just give me a call, all right?"

My heart does that obnoxious squeezy thing again as I watch him hand over his number, and a small smile appears on her lips. This man will be the death of me.

I sling my bag over my shoulder. "Okay, Jordyn, let's blow this popsicle stand!" She smiles over at me and follows me out.

"Did you drive?" She shakes her head.

"I don't drive... I took the bus here."

"Okay, cool, we can take Bethany then!" I open the driver's door and fold the seat forward to throw my bag in the back. Jordyn stops with her mouth open.

"This is yours?"

"She sure is. Her name is Bethany. She's a '76 Camaro and I love her."

Jordyn runs her hand along the frame before opening the door and gingerly sitting. I plop down in the driver's seat.

"Good thing about these old cars, you don't have to be delicate! She's tough!"

Jordyn smiles and I go to put the car in reverse before I realize I don't know where we are going.

"So, what do you feel like? Coffee? Ice cream? Whiskey?" I say the last part jokingly, but she perks up a bit at that.

"Wait... how old are you?"

"I'm actually twenty-three." I must remind myself not to stare, because I'm driving.

"What? No way, I mean... No way!"

She just smiles, and I can see this is not the first time she's having this conversation.

"It's true. I'm just... small, so everyone thinks I'm younger. I think it will be good when I'm sixty, but for now, it just means I keep having to show ID everywhere."

I laugh. "Okay, well, drinks it is. My favourite spot is just down a way. Where do you live? I could drop you off after."

"You can just leave me at a bus station, I'm good." She definitely answers that too fast and drops her eyes. I pull into the parking lot at the pub, but I don't get out right away.

"Jordyn, where are you living?" I take a good look in the back where her bag is. It's a huge duffel that almost dwarfs her. Way more than she'd need to bring just for the gym.

Oh God.

She's living out of it.

She can tell that I've figured it out, too.

"It's not a big deal. I just..."

"Let's go inside and have a drink, okay? We can talk more in there."

When we sit, Juliette is over in a flash. It's quiet still, not quite even the dinner hour. I'm usually here around this time with Twiz, so I know when she gets a look at Jordyn, she's not quite expecting it.

"Hi, Erika! Whiskey with diet okay?" she asks before I even open my mouth. I smile.

"Yes, please, and a food menu. What do you want, Jordyn?"

"Just water for me."

"This is my treat and I'll be insulted if I drink alone," I tell her.

She seems to mull that over for a moment before she says, "A cranberry and vodka, I guess."

Jules looks her over a minute.

"Sorry, pretty girl, but I'm going to have to ask for some ID," she says gently, looking over at me apologetically. I just give her a smile and a nod. I'm happy to see Jordyn has ID, and as long as she's been truthful for me, this will be fun.

Jordyn just nods and pulls a colourful knit wallet out of her backpack, sliding a driver's license from it.

Jules looks it over. "Wow. Happy birthday! Annnd, you're my age. Sorry about that! I would have pegged you for a teenager. I'm usually good at that kind of thing." Jordyn just shrugs.

I look up startled as soon as she says birthday. Jules flips the card back to her.

"This says it's her twenty-fourth birthday tomorrow."

Jordyn just smiles at the table in front of her.

"I guess it is."

She takes her card back and shoves it all into her backpack as Juliette heads off to get our drinks.

"So..." I start, and she finally looks up.

"Here's the thing. It's not a big deal, you know? I just, after the party, I told my parents what happened. I mean, I had no choice. They found me on the lawn... Anyways, they told me that they were sure it was all a 'misunderstanding' and that they wanted me to go with them to see... to see the guys... and make up. Put it behind us. Like they could somehow explain what they did, and we'd laugh, and it would all be okay...

"I just... I couldn't. I'm an adult anyways, I had just been living at home to finish university, so it's not like I had an excuse to have to stay there... They wouldn't let it go. They didn't want to have this 'issue' hanging over us. Turns out one of the guys who... well one of them... his dad works with my dad and our moms are friends... I was so depressed, and I wanted to go to the police, but they kept telling me how I was making it worse by not just moving on.

"So, I packed some of my stuff that I was allowed to take and left. They've never looked for me, so I think they were just glad not to deal with it in the end. I'm sure they told their friends that it just proved that I was the problem.

"I work, part time at a movie theater. I really, really want to try to finish college though. I'm so close and it's already paid for, just a few weeks left. I haven't tried to work full time yet. I haven't been able to save enough for a place with rent and damage deposit with the hours I can work."

"Where are you living, Jordyn?" I keep my voice very low as Juliette discretely drops off our drinks and menus and disappears again.

"Here and there. Over the winter, I stayed with a friend for a bit. She was more of an acquaintance and I didn't want to wear out that welcome. Then I stayed in a shelter downtown for a while, but I hate it there. It's nice out now so I can usually find somewhere comfortable not too far from the school, and then shower at the gym in the morning..." My heart is breaking, picturing this tiny girl sleeping outside before going to classes.

"Jordyn..." She twists her hands uncomfortably on the table.

"I'm sorry. I didn't mean to put this all on you. I'm sure it's not what you wanted when you asked to go out for a drink. I just thought it might be nice to be normal..."

"Please." I put my hand over her tiny ones. "I'm glad I'm here.

94

I'm glad we're talking, too. Thank you for sharing all that with me."

She gives me a timid smile and I hand her a menu., hoping to break up some of the intensity of the exchange. She picks a sandwich once I insist she get something to eat on me, and I ask her a few easy questions while we wait for it to arrive.

"I keep pushing through with college, you know. I have so little time left and I refuse to let them take it from me. I'm almost finished, just exams now, really. I loved working with teams, helping with training, making fitness plans and working with the athletes but now, I can barely walk down those halls in the school. I've just been putting my time in at class and going straight home. I have no idea what I'll do when I graduate."

Jules drops off the sandwiches and hovers for a moment. She's got a funny little multi-colored summer dress on, with knee-high socks and towering heels that she most definitely doesn't have to wear working all day, but I know she loves to anyways. Her hair is poker straight, falling past her shoulders, making me jealous how fast it seems to have come in after she shaved it.

"So... I don't mean to interrupt but just throwing it out there... Now that I've moved to manager here, we've been looking for waitstaff help... It pays pretty decent, and you get to keep your tips, which makes it better than most retail or what-ever. Most shifts are evenings and weekends..." I bite back a smile. Jules is such an adorable little snoop.

It takes a while for Jordyn to get what she's saying.

"You mean me? I've never waited tables before. I don't know if I'd be any good?" Jules just smiles.

"Well, I happen to know the one training you and she's been doing this a while. She's pretty good. I bet you'd catch on." Jules smiles big. Jordyn looks at me and then at her, her mouth in a surprised smile.

"I'm still finishing college, and I'd really like to be sure I do. I have just a couple of weeks left of final exams. But I could come in anytime I'm not there, I swear!" You can tell she's getting excited as she's talking.

"That sounds perfect, Jordyn. I will get you an application form, and we can talk about your first training day when you're done eating. Enjoy!" Juliette skips off and I shake my head. That girl is sneaky. I love her.

"Do you really think… I mean, I don't want them to hire me just because they feel sorry for me." Jordyn picks at her food.

"Juliette just got hired as the manager here after working as a waitress. She really does need someone to replace her. She wouldn't have offered if she didn't want to, she's not like that. You two will get along great. She's a hoot to be around. And that husband of hers." I nod over to Tavish, who's just walking in and shrugging off his leather jacket, placing his motorcycle helmet on the bar. "He's not bad to look at while you're here, either."

Jordyn smiles. "Are all the guys you're friends with that good looking?" she asks, almost like it would be a problem if they were. I remember that I'm talking about a girl who was traumatized not too long ago.

"You don't have to talk about it, Jordyn, but if you do…"

She takes a deep breath.

"It's not that I don't, really. It's just that last time I said anything, they didn't believe me." I squeeze her hand again.

"I promise you. I believe you."

She takes a few more bites of her sandwich and I give her time to decide if she wants to continue, "I had a hard time in school growing up. I'm not crazy book smart. Math and English and all that sitting and reading and everything… After I got held back a year, I lost most of my friends and never quite fit in.

"So, I went to college after school, like everyone does, and just found a general studies program where I barely skirted through for a few couple of years, taking advantage of my parents' college fund, until I found a program where I could learn sports therapy, training and stuff. I was so happy and the first year and a half, I felt like I found a place. My program meant I was always with the school athletes, following around a lot of the teams and such, job shadowing their coaches and trainers. I got to know all the guys, especially, and I was just so happy to fit in. It was different from high school and even though a lot of the players I met were a few years younger than me, I was so excited to have friends who actually invited me to hang out. I never really dated, always felt awkward, but then these guys started talking to me and inviting me places… I loved fitting in.

"I started partying. A lot. I didn't do it at all in high school. I was such a dork then, that I just jumped in so hard. It got to the point I was always out, with parties both nights every weekend. Drinking and using whatever I was given. I thought I was living the best life.

"So, I got invited to a party with some hockey players I had met from school. There were more experienced players at the party, ones from the junior teams, ones with NHL careers ahead of them. The guys I was with wanted to impress them so bad… It was out of control. Every girl I could see was so drunk, people were having sex on the couches in front of everyone. I'd partied a lot, but I'd never been to anything quite that crazy. I convinced myself it was fun.

"One of the others, one of the guys I hadn't come with, brought me a drink about halfway through the night and everything gets fuzzy after that. You probably think I'm an idiot. We all know not to take drinks from anyone, right? I wasn't some high school kid. I was twenty-three! So stupid…"

"Nothing makes this your fault, Jordyn," I say, but she's not really hearing me.

"I remember lying on one of the couches, so tired. The guys I came with, they were arguing with some of the other guys. Then someone picked me up, and after that, it's just a blur. I can see faces in my head if I close my eyes, and I can feel some of the pain because that first guy, he would have been the first to..."

Oh fuck. I take a deep breath, so I don't freak out, and she keeps going.

"Anyways, the next real memory I have is when I was on my front lawn. My clothes were back on, but I had no panties. I was so fucked up in the head. I remember seeing the blood on my legs and thinking they told us in school there wasn't that much blood when you lose your virginity, not like people think. I just stared at it until the pain kicked in, and I realized it wasn't from... they didn't just, I mean..."

Oh. Fuck.

This time I can't just breathe past it.

"Jordyn, I'm so sorry."

She doesn't acknowledge me, lost in the retelling. Her shaking fingers tearing tiny strips of the napkin on the table.

"My parents found me while I was still out there in a daze, and they yelled at me for not coming home that night. I'd never moved out, since they paid my tuition. This way, I didn't have to pay rent anywhere, and they were used to me getting in at all hours in all states, but I always came home. They've never been super attentive or cared much about what I do as long as I went to school and didn't cause them much trouble. But I'm still their daughter, right? I was sure they'd notice, sure they'd be worried about me.

"I told them what happened, and who I was with. Instead of being upset for me, they told me to go inside, take a shower, and forget about it. I couldn't, though. I put on some sweatpants and sneaked back out and went to the hospital.

They patched me up there, I got a few stitches. They took photos and stuff, but I didn't tell them anything. They gave me some medicine and ran all the tests... I have to go back soon to have another one. I've been walking around for months and I don't even know for sure I didn't catch HIV or something...

Anyways, when it was all done, I just couldn't bring myself to talk to the cops they offered to call. The nurses warned me about the questions. Wanting to know what I'd had to drink, what I was wearing, whether I'd been with any of them before, if there were witnesses, all that. I couldn't. I was so tired. So, they said they'd hang on to everything in case I changed my mind. When I got back home, Mom and Dad were on the couch. I thought maybe they'd help, that they'd support me now that they'd had time to think about it. I might go to the police with them backing me up. Instead, they sat me down and when I told them that I'd gone to the hospital, that I was thinking of going to the police, they freaked out. Told me this was all a misunderstanding. That girls shouldn't be hanging out with all boys like I do, that I should have known they'd assume that's what I wanted. They told me that we'd go over to the parents' house of one of the guys and we'd figure it all out together. I just couldn't. So, I left. That was months ago. I never went back, and they've never come looking. Not even at the school and I've been to every class."

My mouth is opening and closing like some demented fish while I try to think of what to say when something catches my eye behind her.

It's Twiz, and he's pissed.

His eyes are wild, the muscles of his chest and arms are tense, pushing hard against his t-shirt. His fists are clenched, and his knuckles are white. Tavish is next to him, the same anger blazing in his eyes. While Jordyn is still looking down at her plate, I catch their gaze and will them to step away. I know they have the best intentions, but the rage on their faces is the last thing she needs. Tav grabs Twiz by the elbow and they head back to the bar.

I have no idea where I go from here, but I'm going to start with Juliette getting me one more drink.

13

TWIZ

*N*o matter how many times I've taught that class, how many women I've seen and known that have been hurt, it never gets easier. I just teach self-defence, I've never heard their stories. Not like that.

Jordyn really, she's just a kid! I was surprised she's even old enough to be in this bar, to be honest. She's quite a bit older than I thought and only six years younger than I am, which is less than the ten or more I thought. I couldn't picture her living on her own though, like it sounds like she is. So, to overhear her story, to hear that a group of little college-boy pussies would hurt her like that, it takes everything in me to walk away.

It takes everything in Tav to get me to walk away, too.

Sitting back at the bar, we don't even say anything to each other. Both of us just stare into our drinks. I've only ever heard bits and pieces of Juliette's story. It's not mine to know, but from what I have heard, I figure this might bring out a lot of anger for him, too. Eventually, he breaks the silence, but his eyes never leave Jules, who's counting inventory behind the bar.

"I was too much of a pussy when we were teenagers, to stop

all the ways Juliette was slowly destroyed by little punks like that. If you find out how…" He lets the sentence hang.

"Don't worry. You're in."

That's all we have to say on it. Both of us are lost to our own thoughts of vengeance, until I see Jordyn a few minutes later head to the bathroom, and Erika walks up behind us. I turn in the barstool and wrap my arms around her instinctively, moving her body between my open knees and holding her against me.

"I don't know what to do," she says into my shoulder, her voice breaking. "She's homeless, Twiz." I freeze.

Behind the bar, Jeremy has appeared. Juliette and he are having a quiet, heated conversation, looking very much like a father and daughter at the moment. I've never really thought it through, but I guess she'd be about that age for him, Jeremy must be close to his forties if not there yet, and Juliette is only in her mid twenties.

"What do you mean she's homeless, Erika?" My outburst gets Jeremy's attention, and I see the set in his jaw. With a quick scowl at Juliette, he heads to the other side of the bar just as Jordyn makes her way out of the bathroom.

Before I even realize it's happening, Jeremy stands in front of her and introduces himself.

"Hi, I'm Jeremy and I own the bar. I hear that you're coming to work for us?" His voice is gentle, and I notice he doesn't touch her or even offer a hand.

"Hi." Her voice is soft, unsure. "I am. I mean, if that's okay, I'd like to…"

"Great! I could use the help. The hours are late, though, and so the position does come with a room and board option. There's an apartment above that's open. I mean, I live on one side of it, but there's a separate living area, bedroom, and bathroom on the other side. I'm not sure if you'd have to break a lease…" I blink a minute, so confused because I know he overheard us say she was homeless, but then I realize he's not only giving her an out but saving her dignity. This way she doesn't think the offer was only for one reason. Even though I'm pretty sure it was.

"I don't... I mean... really? I'm sorry but this is just all so fast and I'm not sure what to say!" Jeremy smiles and Juliette grins like a Cheshire cat, like she's watching some kind of cheesy TV romance. Jeremy lays it on pretty thick with the overprotection, but that can't be it, though, can it? I mean, Jeremy isn't... well... young...

"Tell you what, why don't you give me a minute to sort some paperwork for you, and then we can go up and check it out." Jordyn's eyes widen and Erika steps in.

"I'll go with you!"

"Okay." I think the poor girl is more than overwhelmed but she's smiling. Jeremy leaves, and Erika catches her eye.

"Would it be okay, living with a man like that?"

Jordyn cocks her head as though she hadn't considered that part. "You know, I think because they were so... they were younger than me, I feel almost like... Compared to that guy... to Jeremy... they seem like kids. He doesn't scare me, not like, well..." She looks over sheepishly.

"Not like I do."

"Ya. Sorry."

"Already told you, baby girl, you have nothing to be sorry about." She smiles. Again. I love it.

"I don't think we've met. I'm Tavish." Tav sticks out his hand to Jordyn, but I notice he doesn't get up. Which strikes me at first, because he is usually that kind of traditional polite that reminds me of grandparents at church. Until I realize what he's doing.

At well over six feet of solid muscle, he's trying to make himself seem small.

At least, small*er*.

Jordyn shakes his hand, and Tav gives her one of the biggest grins I think I've ever seen on him. I forget, I think most of us do, the bits and pieces that we know about Jules.

She's shared, mostly on quiet nights here when we've had a few too many and she's forgotten herself, on how hurt she was, how broken. Only ever lasts a moment, though. Tav is always quick to correct her. He never lets her feel bad for however it went for them, and only Silas was there to see. He's not here to tell his tales anymore. That thought gives me a pause and when I look over at Tav I almost feel like somehow, he's followed my train of thought.

I know deep down, though, he hasn't. He just always looks a little like he's just lost his best friend.

That's part of the military he'll never outrun.

None of us will.

I'm brought out of my thoughts when Erika grabs my arm.

"I'm going to bring Jordyn up to see the place. Then I'll... I'll do what she wants before she hopefully lets me leave her here tonight. It might be late, I'm not sure..."

I grab her hip and kiss her forehead.

"I'll be here, Hellcat. Where else would I go?" I give a quick laugh and Tavish does too.

"I'm here late again. Jules is still training new staff so she's working late weekends. I'll keep him company." He bumps my shoulder.

"Tav and I will hang out until you're ready to go."

"You don't have to always follow me back home, you know. I'm okay if you want to go..."

I know she is. Of course she is. I've still been walking her back to her apartment every Friday night.

Truth be told, I've been coming close to walking her back every night since she told me about her stalker. I'm embarrassed about how many times I've sat outside her building or driven by to make sure her car is in the lot underneath. She doesn't take the messages, the threats that she gets seriously. Which still confuses me the more I know her, because she is a control freak. The training, her diet, her apartment, her work. She controls everything, she needs it that way. Yet she ignores the obvious threat on her life.

It… perplexes me.

So, I drive by. I sit by her building and see her light in her window go out before bed.

I try to ignore the fact this makes me close to the same stalker she's trying to avoid.

I don't want to think about that part.

I don't want to think about any part. Not the part that wants to know she's home and safe with the door locked each night. Not the part that wants to move her in with me, so I can be sure every single night.

I don't want to think about any of those parts.

Or what they mean, because they have to mean nothing.

"I know I don't have to, Hellcat. I still will, though."

She smiles.

She fucking smiles like I'm not some creepy, overprotective jerk but like I'm her white knight and for once, I silence that part of me that wants to shut it down. Instead, I let her kiss me.

I let her kiss me like I'm the good guy.

I'm not the fucking good guy.

She disappears behind the staff door with Jordyn, and I feel Tavish's presence behind me before he speaks.

"So, this is a thing, isn't it?" He sits back down on the barstool next to me.

"It's not a fucking thing. I don't do things."

"Does she know that?"

"Of course, you know I never pretend. I was straight with her. She gets it."

Tav looks me over for a minute. He's the youngest of our little group here. Between Matt and Jason and Jeremy and even

Silas before, Tavish was always the youngest. But he was the first to find his place. To find his happiness. Silas had it, but that hardly counts, anymore, not for who we've become since. Jason might be there, we can all see it, but who knows what demons he'll have to overcome to enjoy it.

Fuck knows what's going on with Matt. Jeremy, he's still paying alimony. And it's never in the cards for me. Somehow, that makes twenty-five-year-old Tavish wiser than the rest of us combined.

"You've kept sleeping with her, though. You never do that."

"I don't sleep with her. I don't *sleep with* anyone."

He just shakes his head.

"Semantics. Fine. You're *fucking* her, though. Not just one time, but this whole time. And you're not *fucking* anyone else. That's not like you."

"You're making it a bigger deal than it is. I just found someone where we both like to have sex regularly. We're fuck buddies, no more, no less, and she knows it. I'm not hurting anyone."

"I'll remember that when we're picking up the pieces when it goes south." I snort.

"Erika is a big girl. She'll be just fine."

"I wasn't talking about Erika."

He slaps my back as he heads to the bathroom, and I resist the urge to punch him in the back of his mouthy head.

Fuck.

14

ERIKA

The tour of the apartment upstairs is lengthy, considering it's only a handful of rooms. I think poor Jordyn is more comfortable with the arrangement than I am, and I must dial back this overprotective urge I have to drill Jeremy on all the details and ask her for the five thousandth time if she'll be okay.

She seems to be more than okay, and her behaviour around Jeremy is still timid, but comfortable. She didn't seem to be lying, and she comes across much more relaxed with him than Twiz and Tavish. If anything, Jeremy seems more nervous than she is, reaching to touch her arm then pulling back, showing her each room as though this is a house sale and not a desperate, homeless girl seeing a real bed that she can sleep in safely.

I'm dragging my feet when we're finally done. It's late and while Jordyn never comes out and tells Jeremy she has nowhere else to go, she agrees to stay here tonight. Jeremy gives her a key, some employment paperwork, and a training manual. I leave her in her new room. On my way out, she hugs me.

"I haven't slept in a real bed in so, so long." She smiles with a couple of tears in her eyes, and I have to look away so I don't do the same. I leave her to enjoy the bed, sure that she will probably be asleep before her head hits the pillow.

When I walk out the door of the apartment, I walk right into Jeremy.

"Is she okay? What can I do? Is there something she needs? Should I pick up different food for the fridge? What should I have for breakfast..."

"Jeremy, breathe."

He snaps his mouth closed and looks at me annoyed for a second before his expression softens.

"I just want her to be comfortable."

I look him over for a minute. His head is normally completely shaved, bald and shiny, but it looks like it's been a few days. There's some soft stubble on top that matches what's on his face. I know he's probably close to forty, but his age isn't obvious. The fine creases around his eyes are the only indication. I admit there is more of a calming presence around him than the guys downstairs. Tavish and Twiz, even Matt, their youth and looks are disarming. Maybe even a little intimidating, especially considering they are big guys overall. Jeremy is good looking, there's no denying it, but there's a softness about it. He may not look much older, but he acts like it. Like someone who has nothing he wants to prove. He just feels... safe.

"For whatever reason, Jeremy, she *is* comfortable with you. She's been living on couches and shelters and outside for weeks, maybe months, while still managing to go to the same school as the assholes who hurt her. She's stronger than she looks, so give her that credit. For now, she'll want to sleep. You've given her so much, truly. Thank you."

"What happened to her, Erika?"

Jeremy's voice breaks and the compassion in him for this girl he just met blows me away.

"That's her story to tell. She was hurt, though, Jeremy. Badly. By more than one guy..." His low growl gives me pause but I continue, "So, be gentle, but just remember how strong she's had to be, too."

He nods quickly, his hands in tight, white knuckle fists at his side. I put my hand over one and squeeze, and he relaxes just a little as we head downstairs.

Tavish and Twiz are still at the bar. Twiz is laughing, his head down and eyes on the drink in front of him. When he raises it, he's looking over at Tavish. I take a moment to enjoy the view. The Alexander Keith's t-shirt he pulled on after the gym hugs his chest. With his arms resting on the bar top, the muscles of his forearms bunch as he cracks his knuckles. Pieces of his jet-black hair have fallen forward and has that look as it reaches down his forehead of just being a little too long for his line of work, as though he's just pushing a boundary without crossing it.

Matt arrived at some point and is telling Tavish and Twiz an animated story that has them all in stitches. I'm sure the multiple empty glasses in front of them have helped with their happy mood. Twiz looks up and grins at me, that same disarming smile I know damn well he doesn't realize he gives me. I see Tavish out of the corner of my eye and I know that he saw it, too, if that smirk is any indication.

Juliette comes over with a grin.

"Seems our boys decided awhile ago that a cab was a good idea tonight. I admit it was my idea. We needed to shut down all the testosterone-filled anger that was simmering." I nod. That was probably a good call. Guys like that don't do well when they can't fix a problem like Jordyn's.

"That's okay, I can get mine home," I answer without thinking and the words sour in my mouth. He's not mine, not by a long shot. Jules just grins though. She's just as bad as her husband.

I head over to Twiz's side of the bar and he puts his arm out, pulling me between his legs and resting his head on my chest in front of him.

"I got drunk," he moans, and I laugh.

"You don't say." I step back, and Matt moves over a stool so I can sit next to him.

"It's Juliette's fault. She keeps bringing the whiskey."

"Everyone blames the bartender." Jules winks while she puts a drink in front of me.

"On me, for getting your boyfriend drunk." This is the second time she's jumped there, and I can't bring myself to accept it this time, not in front of him when he would just freak out.

"We're just friends," I clarify, and she just smirks.

Twiz speaks up, "*Special* friends, if you know what I mean."

Juliette fakes a look of contemplation.

"You know, I don't think I do know."

"It means we hang out sometimes, but also I really like her boobs."

I spit my drink and Matt laughs next to us.

"Sure, whatever you say, hotshot." Juliette walks back to her paperwork at the back of the bar and the guys fall back into their drunken banter. It's easy, maybe too easy, the way we talk. The fun that we have. It's something I don't think I've had in as long as I can remember. People who I fall into easy conversation with, who I trust, who I want to be with more than I want to be home with a bath and a book.

It only takes about fifteen minutes after Jules jumps off shift for Twiz, Tavish, and Matt to convince the two of us to abandon all the cars here and take a cab home. Which means I've switched to tequila, and the section has only gotten louder. Jeremy comes and sits with us for a little while too, and as it always does, the conversation moves to military. Jeremy laughs at the old man jokes when they talk about the peacekeeping deployments that took his time before Afghanistan. They laugh equally at 'baby' Tavish as I learn he was only in the military a minute before 9/11 and never saw anything but. Turns out no one is off limits to their merciless tormenting. That can't be clearer than when Jason saunters in.

"Speaking of wimping out on deployment," Tavish says even though no one was speaking of that at all. "This guy didn't even *finish* his last deployment." I stand there, mouth agape, but the rest of them just laugh.

"Whatever. Let me remind you which *disabled tanker* scored better on the last fitness test..." Jason responds, his prosthetic only just peeking from the bottom of his jeans as he pulls himself up on a stool.

Tavish scoffs, "I want a rematch. This time without that damn springy leg you've got there." Jason just smacks him on the back and laughs, and they all fall back into conversation about rucksack marches, tent heaters, and infantry vs armoured, which seems to come up at least once a night every single time they're together.

I'm better off than Twiz when there's last call. His speech has slowed, and his words blend together a little, but his body never sways. We watch the bar staff close up with us inside, and Jeremy's own last call is considerably later. I purposely don't look at the time when Twiz and I are the ones who pile into the first cab together, instead of Matt, who waves us off to crash on Jeremy's couch. We pull up at my place, because hey, if we're going to need to take a cab back to our vehicles in the morning, we might as well make it from the same place, right? It just makes sense.

We have so many explanations for acting like a couple, and none of them are that we just want to be.

We're both in that exhausted stage, past drunk to a more sober, tired buzz, when we make our way to my apartment. Twiz lingers at my kitchen table, and it takes me a second and the look of the wolfish smile on his face, to follow his thoughts.

We're in about the same state as we were that first time, and the memory of him spreading me out on that table like his favourite meal is not one that will ever be forgotten. Before I can even lose myself to remembering, his hands are around my waist and I'm sitting on the edge of the table, with my belt undone as he grabs the fabric at my ankles and pulls. With my jeans gone, he kisses his way back up my thighs, and my head hits the table as I lose myself in his touch.

The light is already peeking through my window by the time we're both in my bed, a little sweaty and completely spent. I'm just drifting off to sleep when I hear his breathy voice from right next to my ear.

"Sure wish I could keep you, Hellcat."

I think, as sleep claims me, that I wish I knew why he thinks he can't.

It's a couple more weeks before it hits either of us how easy this has become. He's here in my bed more often than he's not. He runs with me every Saturday morning, and it always leads to the full day together afterwards. Since we're at the pub every Friday night and always end up in the same bed after, it means we're spending every weekend together.

It's not until a Monday morning almost a month later, we're both in the bathroom brushing our teeth to get ready for work. He had just been explaining how he had to run early so he could get back to his place to pick up his uniform on the way to the base, when he stops almost mid-sentence and catches my eyes in the mirror. It's almost funny the look on his face when the domesticity of our exchange clearly hits him. His toothbrush still in his mouth, the panic in his eyes evident.

"Who knew good sex could last all weekend?" I joke, hoping

to ease some of that panic. It doesn't work. He leans down to spit in the sink.

"Ya..." He's quick to throw his running shorts and shirt on from where they lay on the floor of my bedroom. I don't follow or interrupt. He's already freaked out, and he's not wrong. This was not what we said it would be when we started.

"I've gotta run, but I'll see you next Saturday, right? Probably be busy with work shit before then..." I hear the jingle of his keys and the click of the door opening.

"What the fuck?" I step out of the bathroom and glance down the hall just in time to see him step back inside, holding the door open wide, staring at the other side of it.

Paint is dripping down the front. It takes me a long time to realize it's not a random design because it's begun to blend together into a blob of colour. Eventually, though, it comes into focus. The word WHORE standing out from the mess of still-wet, red paint.

Twiz stares at it a long moment, then back to me. My mouth is filled with mouthwash, I can't even make a sound except the panicked squeak from my throat.

I should have seen this coming.

The messages haven't stopped. Not the texts, even after I changed my number, and not the emails. There's even been two more notes on Bethany after work.

Had I told Twiz any of this?

Hell no.

I'd pretended it wasn't happening and run harder.

Because that's what I do.

Staring at the door now, a drop of acidic mouthwash cutting a path through the foundation on my chin, the idea I could pretend it would just all go away on its own seems ludicrous.

He shakes his head, seeming to clear out wherever his thoughts had gone, and then he's back to me.

"Get dressed, Hellcat," he says, pulling out his phone. "I'm calling the cops." I want to argue but he leaves no room for it, walking to the other room with his phone to his ear. I feel the control slip from my fingers. What frightens me isn't even it leaving, however. It's how easily I'm willing to give it to him.

He's not going to let me ignore this. I only hope he will stick around for however it ends.

15

TWIZ

*H*ell no.

That's my only thought as we sit in silence waiting for the cops to arrive at her place. Since it's not an emergency, it could be awhile, but neither of us has said a word since I called them. Erika just went in her room to get dressed, and I didn't miss the soft click of the door she closed while she was in there. Closing me out while she changed, as though we hadn't just spent most of the last two days naked and entwined with each other. Control. Little slips of control she's trying to infuse in a situation that won't give her any. So, I let her have it.

I know calling the cops shouldn't have been my call, but I've had enough of her ignoring this. The texts and emails and notes, it's like since she can't control it all, she will just pretend it's not happening until it goes away. She doesn't understand that's not how guys like this work. He's not going to just go away. He's going to get worse and worse until the threats are no longer enough.

I know he had to have known I was in here. He was lashing out at my presence in her life. What would he have done if she would have been alone in here last night? I don't even want to let myself go there.

She pads softly out of her room, in a pair of khaki-coloured pants that come just to her mid-calf with a thick belt and soft-white t-shirt. She looks amazing, her bright hair in short, damp waves around her face.

"You can go to work, Twiz. It's okay. I'll wait here for the cops."

"I already called in and let them know I'd be late, Hellcat," I say it casually, as though it wasn't a giant deal for me. I think I shocked the warrant even more than I shocked myself by calling. I'm never late. I didn't even think twice this time.

She opens her mouth but closes it again and instead, just sits next to me on her overstuffed leather couch.

"Where's your laptop? We will need to show them your emails."

She looks at me surprised.

"I deleted all those. Can't we just…"

"I'm sure you haven't emptied the trash folder, though, have you? We're showing them as many of the fucker's messages as we can."

This time she opens her mouth and doesn't think twice.

"I don't think this is your call, Twiz." She stands back up and puts some distance between us. I stop myself from closing the distance myself.

"You're right, it's not. I can't stand here and watch you get hurt though, Erika. I can't. This guy isn't going to stop, and it's only getting worse. I don't know if he's escalating because of me, or some other stupid-ass reason, but guys like him don't back down. He. Will. Hurt. You." I stop when I realize my voice has raised and before I can apologise, there's a knock at the door. Erika keeps her eyes on me as she walks to answer it. A couple of Edmonton's finest introduce themselves, and Erika invites them in.

I stand and shake hands with Const. Taylor, a shorter, stocky-built man in what I would guess is his early forties, with a military haircut and tattoos peeking from the cuff of his uniform when he offers his hand. Const. Marceaux is slight, especially compared to his bulk, her plain-brown hair pulled into a tight ponytail. She's a little younger than he is but both seem confident as they begin to ask Erika questions about the door and the behaviours leading up to it. Reluctantly, after a long glance my way, she heads to her spare room for her laptop to look up the old emails. Curiously, Const. Marceaux follows her and when they are out of sight, the other officer fills me in.

"Most women are more comfortable giving the history of this type of thing with another female. Sheila will take the chance to get the background story while they're in there."

I nod. That makes sense, even if I'm disappointed I won't get to hear it.

"You live here?" Const. Taylor asks, eying my gym shorts.

"No, just stayed last night. Didn't hear anything, though, wish I had."

He asks my name and contact info.

"Infantry?" He nods to my clothes that have my unit on them.

"Yes." He nods.

"I served over a decade with the combat engineers." I give the same nod. We talk for a moment about courses and training and where we've lived, basic Army shit.

"Any way you can make staying here a habit for the next few days while as we look into this?"

I open my mouth to immediately agree without even a thought to the fact that half an hour ago, I was bolting for the door, when Erika comes back in. I'm saved by her declaration that she's found the old emails. The officers look, then ask if she can print them out with her phone records and bring them in to be properly documented. She then takes a card with their info and a promise to get started on a restraining order, which does her little good except start a paper trail to hopefully get this asshole arrested sooner than later.

It's only a few more minutes before they shake hands once more and they're gone. My eyes linger for a moment at the way he puts his hand at the small of her back when they head out the door. It's an easy gesture, but for some reason seems more intimate.

I'm probably reading more into these things than I need to be.

The whole thing took up most of the morning, and we both have to head into work. Instead, we stand for a couple of minutes just staring at each other by the front entrance.

"You don't have to stay..." she starts, but I cut her off.

"I'll follow you into work, make sure you get in all right, okay?"

She opens her mouth, but I don't let her argue.

"That wasn't really a question. I'm going to follow you to work. I'll make sure you get in all right."

She closes her mouth and nods. She grabs her jacket and purse. The walk to my truck is mostly me arguing between the me that was fleeing the domestic bliss I found myself in this morning, and the absolute certainty that I can't let anything happen to her.

Somehow, I need to make that happen without falling any deeper here.

I have no idea how, but I'm going to need to make that work.

ERIKA MAKES an appointment to go by the police station and give over printed copies of her phone records and emails after work, so I meet her there. I don't have to, she sure didn't ask, but here I am, still in uniform after work sitting in the station.

We are soon met by the same two constables that took her statements at the house and she hands over printed copies she'd made of her phone records and emails. She hadn't kept any of the actual paper notes, and I think I bit a hole in my cheek avoiding giving her shit over that, but they write down all the information she gives them about the when and where and what it all said. They then go over all she'd need to file for a restraining order, handing over the paperwork and information on the court she'd file at. It would take a lot of work and I could tell as soon as they handed it to her, Erika had no intentions of following through with it.

She'd be following through.

Erika asks to find the restroom as we are leaving, so Constable Marceaux walks her over, leaving Constable Taylor and me at the front.

"You said you'd be sticking around the next while, right?" He makes direct eye contact and his bluntness betrays his military roots.

"Yes. I'm not going anywhere." I surprise myself with how quickly that rolls off my tongue. A few hours ago, I would have had a very different response.

"As much as we have here, the reality is there's only so much we can do to keep her safe, and I'd wager a guess that spray paint happened because you were in her place when he got there..."

"That's what I figured too. I don't know what he would have done if she'd been alone."

I feel him continue to assess me, but I don't flinch away. It's fair, he wants to know how capable I am, and I know that I have nothing to hide in that regard. I am more than able to protect Erika, and I will.

He finally nods his head, seeming to have found me suitable. "Headed out anytime soon?"

"No, sir. Just got home from Afghanistan not too long ago. Have a little bit before the next exercise, so no plans for anything upcoming. You know how it is, though, can't ever say 100%"

He nods. "I get that." He opens his wallet and pulls out a card for me. "You get called out before we figure all this out, give me a head's up, okay?"

I thank him and tuck the card in my own wallet just as Erika and his partner re-emerge from the hall they'd disappeared. She exchanges cards with them both and the female constable gives her a hug, which seems awkward for both of them. Neither of them come across as the hugging type. We head back to the parking lot and stand in front of where my truck is parked next to her Bethany.

"I'll follow you home."

Again, her mouth is open to argue, and I almost feel bad for how often I feel like I'm interrupting her, but it needs to happen.

Hopefully, she won't just kick my ass to the curb for it. Not that I'm gonna give her a chance.

"Just let me, okay?"

She just nods. I hate how defeated she looks. The spark of my Hellcat is dimmed, it hits me right in the gut. I'm not comfortable with the protective, gnawing feeling it invokes.

I pull up to the parking lot of her complex and run up the stairs. I know she's ahead of me, and I know what she'll see when she gets there.

"What are you guys doing?" She doesn't intend for it to come out as snarky as it does, which is why I did my best to get up here at the same time.

Friendship is something that took me awhile to get used to when I joined the Army, but I've had time to adjust. Erika hasn't... So, coming home to a group of soldiers washing and repainting the door of her condo is undoubtedly more than a little shocking.

"Well, love, we seem to be cleaning up a mess left by some asshole that we will hopefully get to also *clean up* pretty soon," Tavish drawls, and he's met only with stony silence as Erika takes them in.

Tav is closest to her, in an old sweater that looks like it's seen decades of hard wear and a pair of ratty jeans that have flecks of various paint colours on them, none the blue of the door they're currently painting.

Matt is behind, packing up some clothes in a plastic bag. The smell of turpentine is strong on him, and there's a large jug of it behind him. He's dressed much cleaner than Tavish, with a fresh-looking unit t-shirt on top and a pair of clean, almost new-looking jeans underneath. Which doesn't surprise me, I'd actually be more shocked if I found out he even owned anything rougher than that.

Jason is still cutting in the last of the paint at the top of the door, most likely assigned the job being that at a good six foot six and towering even over Tavish, he can reach the top easier than most. He doesn't have a shirt on at all over his low-hanging sweatpants, which I chalk up more to the curious neighbour poking her head out down the hall than any actual heat or fashion choice.

Show off.

There's light-blue paint splatters on the shaved-smooth top of his head, standing in stark contrast to the deep-brown skin.

Matt calls from the other side of the door where he's lifting drop cloths.

"Jeremy would have come but he had to head out for something with Jordyn at the last minute."

Erika still isn't saying anything, she's just staring at the guys while Jason finally throws his brush into a bucket of water and runs his hand across the top of his head, effectively smearing the small drops of paint to sky-coloured smears.

I swallow down my laugh, making eye contact with the others to do the same, because it will be much funnier if we say nothing and let him go home looking like that.

"You guys didn't have to…" Erika starts but I finish.

"No, they didn't, Hellcat. But they did." I give her a moment to process, her thoughts almost visible on her face as they pass.

She wants to know why, and what she owes.

I want to explain to her that this isn't the kind of thing you pay back, but instead, I decide baby steps would be best.

"I bet everyone is thirsty, babe. Have a drink?"

I know she's got some beer in the fridge and chips in the cupboard, so it sounds like it could be a start.

"Yes, yes, of course. I'd invite you in but…" Matt looks up sheepishly from the inside of her door.

"Sorry. We didn't go in, I swear. Just opened it so we could paint." I gave him a key at work, which may have been pushing some boundaries without asking, but I wanted this to get done before she had to see it again.

"Okay." She doesn't even ask how he got in, and I hate it. I want to see the fight back, but the day has just taken it out of her. I give the guys a look. One of the best parts about serving in a war with them is now, I don't need words to communicate with them. They nod, busying themselves with unnecessary tasks outside the door while I follow her in.

"You okay, Hellcat?" It's such a dumb question. I know she's not, but I don't know what else to say.

"Sure." She doesn't look up at me, instead, tidying the already spotless condo. I put my hand over hers where it sits on some ridiculously soft pillow on the couch, moving it one inch to the left.

"Stop." Even close enough that I can feel her breath on my

collarbone, she doesn't look up at me. She just stops what she's doing.

"It's okay that what happened today was not okay. It wasn't okay, and you can't control that." I feel the breath whoosh out of her lungs all at once and her body next to me softens. "I'm sorry this happened, Erika." With that, she completely deflates, burying her face in my neck. Her arms don't move from in front of her and get crushed between us when I wrap myself around her. I feel the little tremors that tell me she's holding back sobs, and I let her because with the guys here, it's not the time. She'll want to let it all go. I'll be there for her then, too, but it's not yet.

After a minute or so, she steps back, her eyes a little red but not wet. A bit of the fire I want to see is back, and I feel weirdly proud that I helped give her that. She turns around abruptly.

"Okay, boys, what can I get you? I have water, beer, and... well, tequila?" She pulls a couple of giant bowls from a dark-wood cupboard and empties a couple of bags of chips in them.

Tav and I grab a beer while Jason and Matt stick with water, and we all sit around the island in her kitchen in silence for a moment.

"Can we talk about how fancy this place is?" Jason is the first to talk, and everyone laughs.

"I'm serious! What is it you do again? I think maybe I need a career change!" Erika laughs, taking a sip of her water. I watch her closely. We've never talked about how she got this place. I'm curious as to her answer. I'm also starting to realize how very little I've ever found out about her.

"I'm an office manager. This place, though, was courtesy of my parents. Well, Dad, really. He put me through college and gave the down payment for here as a graduation gift. I've been lucky that way. Though, I would love to see you behind a desk at an insurance company, Jason, shuffling shift schedules and vacation requests..." Jason makes a face like the very idea makes him sick, and I don't doubt it. All of us cringe at the thought. There's a reason we're soldiers and not accountants.

"Ew. Fuck that. I'll keep my shitty salary, so I can still shoot guns for a living."

I scoff.

"Please. You just drive around…" He gives me a shot to the kidney that my ego won't let on friggin hurt, and we settle into friendly banter for a few minutes while we finish our drinks.

"It's been a long day. Anyone want to stay for pizza? I'm buying."

"Hell, ya you are. Now that we know you're rich in this fancy-ass apartment!" Erika sticks out her tongue and everyone nods their agreement. She reaches for the phone on the counter, stepping out of the room to make the call.

Tavish is, unsurprisingly, the first to speak up. I know this kind of shit pisses him off the most, and it's not lost on me that we were just having a similar conversation about Jordyn not long ago.

"I want a piece of the fucker when you find him," he growls out. The rest all grunt in agreement.

"You said the same thing yesterday. Stand in line." I head back to the fridge for another beer, taking the spot in her kitchen a little too easily, refilling their glasses with their drink of choice.

"Who the hell is he? Just some shit ex, or is it more?" Matt asks. I shake my head.

"You'd have to ask her." I'm not about to tell her secrets, and really, all I know is he was someone that hurt her a decade ago. I'm annoyed with myself now that I don't know more, but I keep giving her privacy, not pushing her. It seemed like the right move at the time but now it just seems like laziness. Was I just not asking because I didn't want to risk the questions that might head my way if I did? All that makes me is a coward.

"Ask me what?" Erika rounds the corner and the guys all

stare dumbfounded and a little chastised for a moment before Matt finally speaks up.

"We were just wondering who the guy is. I mean, other than a stalking douchebag..."

Erika takes a deep breath and goes back to the fridge, reaching up to the freezer and pulling out a bottle of Patron. With her other hand, she scoops a few shot glasses from the shelf above her microwave with a salt shaker and lines them on the island, pouring generously into each one. The guys say nothing. A shot of liquid courage is not something we're unfamiliar with. She licks the back of her hand and sprinkles some salt, the rest of us just wait and when she goes, they each grab one and shoot back with her, the glasses returning to the counter with a bang.

Erika goes to put the tequila back, but instead, just sets it next to the sink before turning to face everyone.

"I guess the easiest explanation of who he was to me," she starts, "is he was step-dad number one."

Tavish's knuckles crack as his fists clench, but there's no other noise.

Her step-dad? The fuck? She didn't tell me that part before. How old was this asshole? How old was she?

"You don't have to..." I start but she raises her hand to me and continues.

"It's fine. I've been pretending for almost a decade that it didn't happen, but it did." She moves to open the fridge, her back to the front of the apartment so she doesn't hear the soft shuffle of steps in the doorway that was left open as the paint dried. The guys and I don't miss it, though, we can't. Before anyone can say something to her, she blurts it out.

"When I was a teenager, I slept with my mom's husband." I'm so proud of the effort that it took for her to get the words out, to accept our friendship and feel safe enough to start to admit her truth as ugly as she thinks it is, that I just so badly don't want her to turn around. Before she can get another word out, she's interrupted.

"Erika?" The middle-aged man in the doorway calls out quietly, and I can almost see the colour drain from her face. I know it before she says it. She freezes, not turning around, just closing her eyes tight like maybe she can pretend he's not there.

"Dad?"

16

ERIKA

*G*od no.

Please tell me this isn't happening.

Nononononononono.

My eyes are still screwed shut. I turn around before opening them to see my pale-faced father standing open mouthed in the entrance to my condo. There's no doubt he heard what I said, it's all over the horrified look on his face.

Shit.

"Erika..." I swear he looks the same way I feel. Desperate to pretend this isn't happening.

I feel Twiz's arm at the small of my back and instinctively, my body leans slightly back into it. He steps ahead, reaching a hand out to my father.

"Hi, sir. It's nice to meet you. I'm a friend of Erika's. My name is Rob, and this is Matt, Tavish, and Jason. We just popped by to give Erika a hand with some home repairs, and she convinced us to stay for pizza." His voice is calm, clear, like he's talking slowly for a child or someone who is new to the language. Even if the sound of his own name sounds strange from his mouth, my dad doesn't seem to notice.

127

Dad stands completely still for a moment, and I'm worried he might not respond at all, but after some tense seconds, he puts his hand out to take Twiz's.

"Hi, Rob. I'm Stewart, Erika's dad. I'm sorry to interrupt. She ran out after work so fast today, I had just wanted to check in..." He lets his sentence hang, and I'm so grateful for the boys who all get up and shake his hand, making quick small talk to fill the empty air.

Matt grabs all the painting supplies. "I'm going to run all this down to my car..." he starts, and they all take the hint, excusing themselves to carry what really one of them could carry alone. Twiz is the last out the door, and he turns, facing me with my dad's back to him and gives me a soft smile before he leaves.

"Dad, look..."

"Why didn't you tell me?" We both start at the same time.

"Right. 'Hey Dad, so, Mom kicked me out after she didn't believe me that her husband convinced me to sleep with him, hurt me, and then wouldn't leave me alone.' Ya, that would have gone over well. Who tells their dad something like that?"

"Erika, you were just a kid... that's not okay! If he raped you, we need to go to the police!"

"I was old enough to consent, Dad. And I did, at least at first. He made me feel special and pretty, and I know now it was all just a game, but he didn't rape me."

This has got to be one of the most awkward conversations in history. I would do literally anything to avoid having to talk to my dad about this.

"What happened after?"

"I didn't want to... I didn't want it anymore after the first time. Hell, I didn't want to do it halfway through the first time. It hurt, and I felt so terrible about myself. But he wouldn't let it go. He kept cornering me, and suddenly, he wasn't nice. He just would tell me how I was fat and he was the only one who would want me like that and I owed it to him for accepting me... When

I finally had the guts to tell him I didn't want to do it anymore, he got violent, and I was scared to be alone with him. I packed a bag just in case and I finally told Mom what he was doing, but she laughed at me. She didn't believe anyone would want to sleep with a chubby girl like me, let alone her good-looking husband. She told me to stop making things up and being dramatic. She said I was just desperate and reading into what wasn't there. That's when I asked to come home."

"Oh, baby…"

"It was a long time ago, Dad. It's not a big deal."

I hear a cough and look over to see Twiz standing just inside the door. I really need to stop letting people sneak up on me in my own home. He's not going to let me drop it, damn him.

"Fine. FINE. I've gotten some… messages. He's been bugging me at work and on my cell. It's okay now, though. I'm taking care of it, and I've gone to the police. They'll talk to him and he'll stop. He's a coward. He'll let it go once he knows he could get in trouble." I lock eyes with Twiz, willing him to let that be enough. I don't want to worry my dad more than I need to, or I'll never get rid of him. He's smothering enough without the excuse of protecting me.

Dad is quiet for a long moment and then takes a deep breath, letting it out slowly.

"I'm so sorry, Erika."

"This wasn't your fault, Dad."

"I never should have let you go live with her. I should have known…"

"Dad. There was nothing you could have done."

"If I would have known, I never would have continued to encourage you to have a relationship with her! Erika, I never would have…"

"Dad. It's over. It wasn't your fault and you didn't know. I don't blame you."

I can tell he has a hundred more questions but Twiz finally

makes his presence known behind him as I hear the others coming down the hall. Instead, he comes around the counter and gives me a hug. I look over his shoulder at Twiz who is somehow with his expression telling me what I don't want to do.

"Do you want to stay for pizza, Dad?"

He steps back with a look on his face like he won the lottery. I never eat pizza, and I rarely spontaneously invite him over since he's usually consistent about inviting himself.

"I would love to, honey, as long as your friends don't mind."

"Hey, it's free pizza. We'll eat free pizza with anyone!" Jason pipes up, and everyone settles on the couch. Conversation moves to various small talk topics like the weather and their work. The guys are all vague with their answers but encourage Dad to tell them all about his company. Which doesn't take much encouraging at all, and by the time the pizza arrives, they know more than I'm sure they ever wanted to about the insurance broker industry.

I throw on the TV to some reruns of Friends once we're all settled with our plates and the distraction works. We all eat in companionable silence for a while. When I get up to put my plate in the sink, Twiz comes up behind me, I feel his presence before I feel him. His chest presses up against my back at the sink.

"You didn't even finish one piece of pizza, Hellcat."

"It seemed like a good idea at the time, but I can't eat that many calories like this. I didn't even get out for a run today."

He takes a moment where I feel his breath against the sensitive spot just below my ear.

"You could. I'm all about eating healthy and staying in shape, Erika, but sometimes it's okay to have pizza."

"Not for me, it's not."

A low growl vibrates through my body from his and I feel it even more than I hear it.

"Erika, you're hot as fuck. But girl, you'd be just as hot with five more pounds on you. Or twenty. It's not healthy to worry so much. I heard what you told your dad and all this control. It makes more sense to me now. We're going back to this, you and me."

I close my eyes, determined not to let him see how his words affect me. It took me too much work to get here, I don't want to hear it. I twist in his grip so I'm facing him.

"I like myself like this, Twiz. That should be enough."

"Of course it is, Hellcat. I don't get to tell you how to look, that's all you. And for the record, you're rocking it. I just wish you liked yourself no matter what."

I don't have an answer to that, so I busy myself with wiping the counter instead. He lets it go, probably because the conversation behind us is picking up again, and my dad uses that moment to speak up loud enough so we all hear.

"You... you're missing a leg!"

I drop my head and shake it, my eyes closed tight. Twiz snickers beside me. I look up to see Jason, who's got his legs up on my coffee table, the sleek metal of his left one just now becoming visible below the cuff of his jogging pants, grinning. He responds with what I can only assume is his best sincerely surprised voice as he pulls his pant leg farther up and knocks on the exposed prosthetic.

"Ho-Lee shit. You're right!" At that, the rest of them can't control their laughter, and my dad seems to find his sense.

"I'm sorry, son. That was rude of me. I don't know where my manners are. Caught me by surprise is all."

Jason gives a good-natured shrug. "S'all right. Catches me by surprise sometimes, too."

"That happen in Afghanistan?"

Jason is quiet for a moment and I worry again my dad is asking too much of him. He speaks up eventually, though.

"Yes, sir. IED in 2007. Hit it in the tank, blew right through

131

the bottom. It's a papercut, though. I still have my knee, this just makes me a little bionic. Still kick their ass in a race any day." He shrugs in the direction of the others who just shake their heads with a grin. From what I've heard, he's not joking.

I'm actually surprised how my dad just nods, taking it in, and then says, "They find the fuckers that did it?"

I sputter the wine in my mouth, and it sprays a fine mist on the counter in front of me. Twiz looks over with a bewildered look. I think that's the first time I've heard my dad use that language in my life. Jason and the rest, however, just laugh.

"Oh yes, sir. My squadron tracked down the insurgents likely to have set the bomb and tell you what, I bet they were *really surprised*." He makes an explosion noise and splays his fingers out in front of him.

"Nothing like watching the leopards blow a hole through the enemy," Matt muses, shaking his head.

"Ha! I knew it. You fucking *wish* you were tankers!" Jason is almost giddy. Matt throws his pizza crust at him and they settle back into conversation. I stand with my mouth open at my dad's apparent ease in fitting in with these men.

I don't know that I've ever given him much a chance to be part of my life, really. I see him plenty, but never have I let him interact with the people that make up my life. Not like this.

Turns out, he's all right.

Who knew?

It's not too much longer before my dad stands and says his goodbyes. It's a Monday night, after all, and pushing ten o'clock by now. Normally, I'd be well past bedtime at this point, ready to get up at five to head for a run. On his way to the door, Dad stops and hugs me again, this time with a little less urgency but the same ferocity.

"I am so, so sorry you felt there was a time you couldn't come to me. I'm going to do better, Erika. I'm so sorry."

I don't want to tell him again that it's not his fault. That he was so broken from what Mom did, I couldn't add more. That I was embarrassed and didn't want him to see that insecurity.

I don't want to get into how instead, I threw myself into weight loss and running and calorie counting and control.

So, instead, I say nothing. I just hug him back harder and for once, let him hug me until *he* is done instead of pulling away. He leaves, assuring me we will talk again in the morning, which I dread since I don't want to bring this into work. I don't correct him because I'm just grateful he hasn't made this a bigger thing than it is here, in front of the guys.

Soon Jason saunters out from the bathroom, muttering about everyone letting him walk around with baby blue paint smeared on the top of his head, and with that him, Matt, and Tavish bringing their plates and garbage to the kitchen and say goodbye, refusing to accept any more than a quick thank you for their work. When the door closes behind them, it's just me and Twiz.

He lets me put all the dishes in the dishwasher, wipe down the counters, and even prepare my breakfast and coffee for the morning before he says anything.

"It's late, Hellcat. Let's go to bed."

I look up confused, because he said 'let's.' That's when it registers that he's changed. He's in shorts and a t-shirt instead of the uniform he was in when we got here. I don't even remember when he did that.

"You don't have to…"

"I'm your shadow until further notice. Until the police figure all this out, you're going to have to put up with me. I've got a bag with me. I promise I won't make too much of a mess." He's using that same slow, controlled voice that he used before, like talking to a child.

I want to argue but I don't. I can't. The truth is I've had so much control ever since I became an adult. The whole time I've lived on my own. I can't imagine living without it, and I'm terri-fied. I don't want to sleep alone.

I just nod. I guess not saying what's on my mind and instead, just saying nothing at all seems to be my go-to right now. We quietly go about an awkward routine of bedtime, taking turns in the bathroom, setting alarms, preparing tomorrow's clothes. Mundane activities that only add to the domesticity of things.

This morning, when he bolted to the door, seems forever ago, and it's hard to imagine the man setting out his socks in my bedroom is the same guy who looked at me like I had tried to throw a wedding ring at him only eighteen hour ago.

"What's on your mind?" He grins at me and I realize I've been staring at him lost in thought.

"Just running through my day tomorrow," I lie, and he lets me.

We both crawl into the bed, Twiz stopping part way.

"You know, I never asked if this was okay. If it's too much, I can sleep on the couch. I don't mind."

I just stare at the gorgeous planes of his chest and abs and wonder how he thinks I would ever turn down having him in my bed.

"Just get in, Twiz." I slide between the sheets, the exhaustion I've been teasing with all day sitting heavy on my head as soon as it hits the pillow. He gets in too, lying on his back awkwardly as though he doesn't know which way to move his body.

We've fallen asleep in this bed together dozens of times at this point, but it occurs to me that it's never been just a comfortable, routine moment, but always after heated passion and sated exhaustion. He's completely out of his element, his body stiff as a board and his breath coming in strange, almost forced movements that I feel even without touching him.

I'm too tired to help him work through whatever's going on for him. Instead, I let him process it all himself, not sure if he'll still be there when I wake up but too exhausted to make him promise me.

I make the consequence tomorrow's problem as I drift off to sleep, only vaguely realizing how badly I want him to stay, and how devastating it will be when inevitably, one day he doesn't.

17

TWIZ

*I*t's still quiet on the training grounds, and my rifle in front of me should feel like an old friend. Instead, I stare at it as though it was, once, but has since betrayed me. I can't pick it up, and that's a problem. So, I stare at it, willing myself to remember the complete feeling of having it in my hands, instead of the burning fear simmering in me.

This can't be happening. I won't let this happen.

I have soldiers arriving soon that I'm supposed to instruct. Like I've done so many times before, this should be easy. I pick up the rifle. It should fit easily in my hands but instead, it's clunky and awkward. It's an extension of me, but now it feels like one that was amputated and replaced differently, no longer offering a seamless fit. I used to feel my heartrate slow when I held it, feeling the calm I needed to make the shot. Now, I feel it race, it's this unfamiliar feeling of my heart in my throat that I can't seem to swallow.

I put it back down and stare at it again. Every blink is the face of that girl, the fear in her eyes and the jerk of her body when my shot hit. I stare at my hands. They look the same as always, which doesn't make sense to me. There's so much blood on them and I don't remember cleaning them off.

I just need a minute. I close my eyes but it's worse, I can hear Tav in my head but this time he's telling me not to shoot. Yelling at me that she's just a girl, that there's another way.

I shoot anyways, the rifle jerks in my hand.

I open my eyes.

Why are my hands clean? I search them for the blood, but it's all gone. Why? Who cleaned the blood off? Why would they do that, knowing what I did.

I don't know what's worse, closing my eyes and seeing her face, or opening them and realizing the blood is off my hands.

I startle at the sound of Matt's voice behind me. It takes me a minute, it should only be Tav here on the berm with me. Everyone else is in the valley below, talking with the village elders, but they're not... because I'm at the range in Alberta, not the hill in Afghanistan.

I didn't hear him approach.

I always hear someone approaching.

"Hey, Twiz." The pity in his tone grates down my spine. Can he see my heartbeat? He's still a couple of steps out, his hand in front like he's trying to tame a wild animal.

"You didn't need to come out, I'm good."

"Twiz, the troops called me. They've been here awhile."

I look up from where my rifle sits on the grass in front of me, and I see a group of privates and corporals, the soldiers who were slated to run through the range with me today, staring from the edge of the field.

I look back at Matt.

"There's no blood on my hands."

His shoulders sink. "No, Twiz, there's not. You haven't done anything wrong."

He doesn't see the blood, either. Did he wash it off? How did I let that happen?

"You don't understand, her blood was there! Someone has washed it off and it's not fair, people need to see it. They," I gesture to the soldiers milling around, pretending not to listen, "need to see it, so they know what I did to her."

Matt takes another few steps towards me and bends down. I realize he's trying to take the rifle from me but slowly, like I'm a spooked horse he doesn't want to startle.

"Go ahead, take it. I can't figure out how to shoot the damn thing anyways." I step back from it and his face relaxes as he picks it up.

Once it's in his arms, I see him motion to pass it to someone else. It's Lt. Froese. I didn't see him coming, either.

Fuck.

Matt doesn't turn his back to me, passing the rifle behind himself where the lieutenant grabs it, and then taking another step forward.

He doesn't turn his back to me.

He's scared. Of me.

FUCK.

"How long have I been out here?" I ask the grass, my hands still in front of me, suspiciously clean. It feels like five minutes, but I wasn't expecting the troops for another hour.

"Almost two hours, Twiz."

At that, I look up at him, his eyes squinted, blinded by the sun, his pupils hiding in the ice blue. He's not wearing sunglasses. He always wears sunglasses, only taking them off when he's worried or focused.

"It didn't feel that long." My voice is a hoarse whisper that grates on my nerves. "Sorry, we're running late. Just... I'll get these guys started right away, okay?"

"Let's not worry about them. Why don't we head back down to battalion and talk?" His voice is clear, punctuating every syllable the way you'd speak to a child. I hate every sound out of his stupid mouth.

"No. I need to finish work here." I'm not leaving. I'm not letting them write this down, make out like I couldn't do my job. I can do my damn job. I just need a second.

"Twiz, I need you to come back with me, okay? Sgt. Michaels is going to run the range today."

What? No. I'm not being replaced. I'm not letting them pull me from this. That's how it starts and then you end up on the other side, a soldier who can't do their job. Fuck him for trying to make me that guy over one bad morning.

"I'm not crazy, *Captain Christianson*. I need to run these troops through the training. I'll be fine."

Matt appraises me, and the look on his face almost has me back down. He'd scare ninety percent of the troops out there with that look, but we've been friends too long. I know pulling out rank like that was a douche move, but he *is* my boss. My *friend* wouldn't make me do this.

"I'm not asking, *Sergeant Sampson*. Let's go."

We stare at each other for a minute before I drop my eyes and follow. I try to hold my head up as I walk past the troops waiting in the wing, but in the end, I look away, towards the vehicle in the distance, like the failure I am.

We make it back to battalion in silence and in all that time, I can't think of what you call a soldier who can't pick up his rifle, other than not a soldier at all.

BY THE TIME the day is done, I am too.

They pulled me from my platoon.

Sure, they say it is just temporary while I figure things out, and they moved me up with Matt to help plan the training and other operational administration that doesn't require I hold a rifle for a while, but I've been around too long not to see the writing on the wall.

If I can't move past it, I'm done.

I'm done.

Two words that have been playing on my head in a loop since I left the BSM's office.

Sure, all they said was things like 'mental health services' and 'time to process things' and 'nothing to be ashamed of,' but that's all bullshit. There's a laundry list of things I should be ashamed of, and there's no such thing as an infantry soldier who can't pick up a rifle.

Worse than that, no matter how hard I search in myself, I don't see how there's such a thing as me if I'm not an infantry soldier.

Which means I have very little time to figure this out and get my shit together, so I can prove this was a one off and I can have my platoon back.

I also have an appointment with base mental health next week. This is only because I managed to convince them I didn't need to go to some emergency commitment today.

Matt hasn't looked at me since he pulled me from the range. I've been in and out of meetings before I was eventually told to go home, once they decided I wasn't a danger to myself. Which seems laughable to me, since I can't pick up a damn weapon anyways, apparently. I walk by Matt's office, trying to get out of there without having to see him, knowing damn well I live with him so I'm not sure how long I think I can avoid him. He catches me as I make my way past his door.

"Sergeant, can you come in here a second?" His voice is light and doesn't betray which I can only assume has to be the stress behind it, after his best friend just lost his shit while trying to hold a rifle at work. I step in his office and stare at him a moment, and he holds my gaze. I know he wants me to really talk. It takes me a while before I concede, closing his door and sitting down. He comes around from the other side of his desk, something he only does when he's trying to be my roommate instead of my boss.

"What happened out there, Twiz?"

I swallow. "Nothing. I'll figure it out. It's not as big of a deal as they all think. I can do my job..." Matt cuts me off.

"Fuck off. It's just me right now, okay? Drop all the bullshit you've been giving the rest of them."

I take a deep breath. "Really, it's just this one time. I'm sure it was..."

"It wasn't the first time. You had a panic attack at home, too." I let the silence stretch. That wasn't even about the deployment, but I'm not about to tell him that. It's also the first time in years that it's happened, so now I'm not so sure. I think about my overreaction in the park with Erika and the plastic bag awhile back. The few times I've been stuck in the truck, trying to count down to make my heart stop racing. I think of the sight of all the blood on me when I first put my uniform back on. This wasn't so much of a one off as I'd like it to be. I lean my head back on the chair and close my eyes.

"I need this job, Matt." I hate the desperation in my voice.

"No one is throwing you out, Twiz. Just take a minute..."

He's not wrong. If some deep-down part of me wasn't sure this was a bigger issue than just today, I wouldn't be panicking over this. I need to play it cool, take a moment and come back stronger so they have faith in me again. I stand.

"You're right. I'm going to head home. Maybe I just need a break." Matt's eyes are hard, and I know he sees right through me, but I'm hoping he'll decide now's not the time or place to push me.

Thankfully, he does. Standing, he gives me a quick shoulder hug, talking to my ear before he lets go, "I'm not letting you get pushed away, Twiz. You have to trust me."

Smacking his back and stepping away, I leave his office before there's more emotion in the room than I'm ready to deal with. Walking out to my truck, I try my best to ignore the looks from everyone I pass. It feels like the three-minute trip takes twenty, and I all but collapse in the driver's chair when I get there, my heart racing far more than it has any right to be.

I take deep breaths as I remind myself what day it is. It's Friday. Erika is working and then headed to the gym. I said I'd meet her there, but there's no way. There's no way I'm doing anything, really. Except what I'm doing right now, which is stopping at the liquor store on the way to our place and grabbing a bottle of Black Velvet. I don't even grab a bottle of Coke to go with it.

I haven't been home to my and Matt's place in a week, but that's where the car brings me this time. I pull into the driveway and the last smart choice of my night is to grab my phone, using the text for once. I send a message to Matt. Someone needs to meet Erika and stay with her tonight so she's safe.

It just can't be me.

By the time I make it inside, I'm a wreck. My face is wet, and I'm only more disgusted with myself about it. I head inside, flopping down on the couch and opening the bottle of whiskey without changing or even thinking to grab a glass.

I sit in complete silence for the first few pulls of the golden liquid, letting the sting in my throat and the burn in my stomach keep my focus. It doesn't take long before the edges of my thoughts go fuzzy, and comforting numbness gives me the temporary reprieve I need from the reality I'm cowardly running from. It's almost enough, but not quite. I take another swig, putting my feet up on the cheap coffee table and flipping on the TV in front of me. I don't even see what's on, just let the noise of the tinny speakers break into the background of my thoughts, willing them to muddy it all enough that I can't feel the hurt.

The home phone rings more than once but I don't answer, watching the flash of the voicemail light on the receiver next to my feet as it blinks, willing me to care. I don't, though. I'm guessing it's one of the guys, and since Matt will have told them to find me, I know it won't be long until they do, but it's still early in the day. They'll all still be at work.

So, I'm not as surprised as I should be when the door opens without so much as a knock and Tavish walks in. He's in his gym shorts and t-shirt, his hair still a little damp with sweat. If I wasn't so pissed off at having to deal with him, and at Matt for sending him, I'd be impressed with how fast he obviously left after sports this afternoon. He takes a good look at me before plopping down on the couch.

"Fucking hell, Twiz."

I pass him the bottle, but he shakes his head.

"I've spent enough time on couches feeling sorry for myself with a bottle. Besides, that shit is fucking nasty."

I snort. "Snob."

He just shakes his head. We sit in silence for a while, yet he doesn't try to take the bottle or even get me glass. He just sits next to me, after a while grabbing the remote and flipping channels aimlessly.

Eventually, his silent presence pisses me off.

"Don't you have somewhere to be, Tav?"

He just shakes his head.

"Jules is hanging out with Beth tonight. Jason has some amputee support group shit or something and apparently, Matt is heading over to your girlfriend's house because you're here."

"S'not my girlfriend." I surprise myself with the slur in my voice and take a look down at the half-finished bottle and shrug.

"Sure. Fine. Erika's house. Your 'not' girlfriend."

Nothing else is said for a little while longer. Eventually, I cave.

"Why are you here?"

"Why not?"

"Maybe because I didn't invite you?"

With that, he laughs a little and drops his head to his hands, rubbing his temples with his thumbs.

"This is painful. I really owe Jason…" I have no idea what he means. Eventually, he looks back up.

"I'm not as patient as he is, and I won't watch you destroy yourself for months. You're better than this, Twiz."

That's enough to make me laugh this time.

"Oh ya? You're still here. So's Matt, and even Jason. Fuck! Jason most of all. And yet, here I am, and I can't even pick up my rifle, Tav. All I could think all morning while I stared at it was that someone washed the damn blood off my hands."

"We all have blood on our hands, Twiz. All of us. None of it wasn't justified."

"You could see as well as I could that the girl didn't want to do it. She probably didn't even understand what it was. She was just some innocent they used to get to us, and I blew her damn head off."

"You saved the lives of our platoon."

"Right. And I'd do it again. So, what does that make me if not a murderer?"

"It makes you a fucking soldier, Twiz."

I'm breathing heavy at this point, and my face is wet. Again. I can't remember the last time I cried, and this is twice in one damn day.

"Just because you had a bad day…"

"It's more than that," I admit. I don't *want to* admit it, but my thoughts are muddled from the whiskey and my self-preservation is all but gone. I'm tired of lying.

"It started with little things, you know, stuff that happens to most of the guys a time or two. I was jumpy, saw danger where there wasn't, had trouble sleeping. Usually that stuff just takes time to settle after I get back. But it's not getting better, like the other times. It's getting worse. I keep having panic attacks, and not just about work stuff." I think of the morning I freaked out over the news and Matt had to talk me down. "I didn't want to admit that's what they were, but it is. I went in early today to the range because I knew. I haven't even been able to look at a rifle since we got back. I knew I wouldn't be able to pick it up. Tav, I didn't even see my guys on the range. I have no idea where my head went, but I was gone for hours. Hours. With my loaded rifle right in front of me."

"You can get help for this, Twiz." I hate how calm his voice sounds.

"I know, Tav. But I also know, somehow, that this is it. I might get better, but I'm not going to get better *enough*."

"You can't possibly know that by now…"

Now, my voice is the one that's calm. Resigned. The drink has settled into a comfortable buzz and even more than that, so has the truth.

"Ya, I can."

Tavish says nothing to that, and we go back to quiet as I finish the bottle in my hand, and he doesn't even try to stop me. I get that. There's unspoken understanding that he's going to let me have this, but it also seems he's not going to let me do it alone.

Eventually, he orders pizza and we throw on a movie. He doesn't make me talk about it anymore and I don't. Finally, when the last credits roll, he stands.

"Twiz, you're not doing this alone, okay? No matter what. Whether you're in or out, we're not going anywhere."

I avoid his eyes, looking anywhere but. He eventually grabs the pizza box, throwing it in the garbage before heading to the door.

"Tav?" He turns, and I hate the weight I see on his shoulders, knowing I put it there.

"Thanks, man. I'll be good. Thanks for hanging out."

He just nods and closes the door behind himself. I stare at it for a while, almost willing him to come back and save me from being alone. Eventually, I get up and head to the kitchen. My whiskey is all but finished, but I find another half-full bottle on top of the fridge and drag it back to the couch with me. I still haven't changed, but I don't bother at this point.

As my eyes close, I see Erika's in my mind, the way they melted into mine when I take her. I'm reminded of something Tav told me once, about some old love song with sappy lyrics singing of seeing your unborn children in your woman's eyes. He told me he'd never thought twice about it until he looked at Juliette.

As I drift off, sitting upright on the couch, I see her soft green eyes change, I see a child in her arms become one on her hip; the heartaching beauty of the love in them gazes up at me.

Love that turns to fear. When a hand that I know is mine but looks too much like my father's lashes angrily towards them.

I see their tears and their bruises.

I see their blank stares and all the blood.

I jerk awake, sweat pooling down my back, feeling like I'm sinking, suffocating on the cushions.

Everything might be a mess, and I have no idea where I go from here, but one thing is sure. More so now, without the promise of the Army to keep me in line, my only next step is to let her go.

I get up off the couch and grab my keys and the bottle off the table.

It's time to see this through, while everything is numb enough to let me.

18

ERIKA

His truck is there when I pull up just after six Saturday morning.

Part of me is relieved. I'd been worried when I saw Matt at the gym and confused when he told me he was crashing on my couch last night. He told me Twiz had something come up at work, but I didn't quite believe him. He wouldn't look me in the eye. Instead, he just worked out in the weight room while I took my fitness class, then followed me back to my place. He spent most of the night on his work phone, insisting on ordering and paying for his own Chinese food when I made myself a stir fry. I finally relented when I realized no amount of convincing that I was fine would get him to go home. We watched a ridiculous made-for-TV rom-com before I padded off to bed, leaving him and his camouflage blanket and pillow on the couch.

Matt had stared at me incredulously when he awoke to me in the kitchen making coffee at five thirty this morning, and flat-out choked when I told him my plans for the thirty kilometers today, but he still wouldn't let me head out alone. He grabbed the gym clothes from his bag and headed to the bathroom, mumbling how bad Twiz would owe him one under his breath. His car pulls up behind Bethany when I get to the River Valley, and when I catch a look of Twiz behind his giant truck, I'm glad he's there.

"Heyyyyy, Hellcat!" Sitting on the pavement, leaning against his back bumper, is a very rough-looking Twiz. His hair is sticking up all over his head. There are dark circles under both eyes, and the hint of scruff on his unshaven face.

"Shit." Matt jumps out of his car, coming around back.

"And Captain Christianson! Fancy seeing you two here!" Twiz attempts to stand, but the hand on his bumper slips and he slides back down onto the damp ground, laughing humourlessly at himself. Matt stands in front of him and puts out a hand, but Twiz swats it away frustrated.

"I don't need your fucking help, Captain. I'm just fine." He slowly pulls himself up to standing before almost immediately leaning back on his tailgate and dragging an almost empty 26 of whiskey to his lips. The bottle looks as rough as he does, with the label picked off and the glass scuffed like it's been rolling around on the pavement all night.

"I knew you'd be here. Never miss a week, right? Always follow the training, follow the plan. Your perfect house, perfect body, perfect schedule. Perfect Erica." He spits the last words at me, clearly meaning them more as an insult than anything else. I start to fight him on it, but he almost completely misses his mouth with his swig from his bottle and he looks so pathetic. I can't even bring myself to bother.

"C'mon, Twiz, let me take you home." Matt puts his arm back out to him, but Twiz flinches from his touch again, and I wonder what really happened between these two yesterday.

"Nah, I think I'm gonna stay right here. Maybe I'll go run with *my* girl, and *you* can go home? Hey?" I take a good look at him and realize he's still in his work clothes. The camouflage uniform pants and a green t-shirt on top, the button-up shirt laying on the ground where he had been sitting, his name just visible on the top of the heap. I try to focus on how bad of a sign that is, instead of where my heart wants to focus—the fact he called me *his girl*.

"Twiz, you're fucking lucky that you haven't already been arrested out here. You get busted for DUI or public intoxication, especially in uniform like this, and I won't be able to make that go away. C'mon. Let me take you home." Matt's frustration starts to show, but his voice is still calm, slow. He's standing with his hands in front of him like he's talking to a rabid animal.

"I was much sobererer... er... I wasn't so drunk when I drove here. I even put the... put the open bottle in the back of the truck. So there."

Matt just shakes his head. "You might have been in better shape then this but driving drunk is still a dick move, Twiz."

"I wasn't drunk when I was driving!" This time, Twiz yells but Matt stays rigid.

"Ya? Would a cop believe you? You blow over and you lose your damn license and cause even more of a go at work."

"You'd all like that, wouldn't you? That would be proof that I'm crazy, wouldn't it? 'Look at Sgt. Sampson. Just another drunk soldier, too weak to handle war. Lost it, now he can't even pick up his damn rifle. Sad, sad, case, isn't it?'" He makes this exaggerated tut tut noise before taking the last swig from the bottle in his hands, looking at it and tossing it in the bed of his truck. "Did you tell her? Huh? Did you tell her how pathetic I was?" He motions over to me, the force of moving his one arm in my direction causing his whole body to move and he takes a step towards me to steady himself.

"You wouldn't do that, would you, Matt? Goody two shoes Matt, practically a priest, you wouldn't do anything like that. Well, I will." He looks at me, his bloodshot eyes glaring into mine. For the first time, I am not struck by the beauty of the contrast between the blue and brown, yet I'm distracted by the emptiness of his stare.

"I'm useless. I couldn't even pick up my fucking rifle yesterday. There I was, supposed to teach the soldiers on the fucking range, and I couldn't even pick up the fucking rifle. Ironic, huh? I shot some poor girl and now I can't pick up my rifle. So, where does that leave me? A killer, that's what it leaves me. A killer who can't do the only job he's good at. Useless." He spits the last word at the ground and lets himself crumple back to the pavement. Somehow, with his knees up at his chest, he looks small. Matt moves forward to him, but I put my arm out to stop him, instead stepping to him myself. He glances up at the sound of my footsteps and his look turns desperate for just a half second that I almost miss before it becomes cruel.

"I sent my best friend over to watch you, so how good a job did he do, huh? Is he as good as I am? Did you open your legs as fast for him as you did for me? Hey? I hope so, I mean, that was the whole *fucking* idea." I stand stunned, and he flits his gaze over to Matt. "You were smart enough to fuck her, right? Hope you got a taste, too, made it good for her... Do you even know how? Can you make her scream like I can? Doubt it. You wouldn't hurt her, though. So, I'm sure you'd learn eventually..." His voice almost trails off at the end, as though he's already ashamed of the words he's spoken but he can't take them back.

"Fuck you, Twiz." It comes out as a whisper and doesn't have the venom I wish it did. I can't seem to stir up the vitriol that his outburst should cause. Instead, there's nothing but this painful, empty hurt. It's so much worse.

"That's enough!" Matt's outburst startles me when it comes from behind. The fierceness in his words sends shivers down my back. I've never heard him use that tone before and I can, for just a moment, see the boss they've told me he is. I can almost imagine him in charge when usually, I just see the quiet one of the group, the one who gently seems to hold them all up without being seen himself.

"Oooooh," Twiz lets out in sarcastic shock, a sneer on his

face. "I guess it's Captain Christianson again. Well, guess what, Captain? I'm not one of your troops. You. Don't. Scare. Me." He pauses on each word, his eyes boring into his best friend's. I look behind me and only just catch the moment of hurt on Matt's face before he puts the mask back on, lunging forward and grabbing Twiz under his armpits before hauling him to his feet.

"I'd be more pissed off if I didn't know how much you're going to hate yourself in the morning. You might not give a shit about what you say to me, but I'm not going to let you talk to Erika like this. You want to feel sorry for yourself? Do it without hurting your girl and preferably without ending up in jail. I'd rather not deal with the paperwork. You're better than this, Twiz."

The fight seems to leave Twiz and he slumps over, letting Matt haul him to his car where he all but throws him in the backseat. He doesn't argue, or even make a sound, just lets his head hit the window and closes his eyes. I hear him whisper something like "She's not mine," before Matt shuts the door and looks over at me apologetically. I wave him off. I don't want any more pity. It's embarrassing enough that he saw all that. Heard all of what Twiz said to me. Then, I remember how Twiz accused him of sleeping with me, basically accused me of being a whore, and I feel my face heat up. Which just makes me angrier. I haven't felt guilty about enjoying sex in a very long time.

"I'm so sorry…" I don't know what else to add, but Matt cuts me off anyways.

"You have nothing to be sorry about. He's going to regret that in the morning. Well," he glances at his watch, "later today, I suppose." He chuckles under his breath, but he sounds about as happy as I feel, and his laugh is dry.

"Look, I know you're supposed to be going for a run…" I had almost forgotten. I don't want to give up my miles, however. My race is too close to be letting my training go. I feel the itch, the deep need in my gut to go, to run, to keep going and push myself to exhaustion so I can forget. I know I won't give up my morning for him.

"It's okay. I'll stick to the city roads. I hate running through town because of the lights, but I will this time so I'm not down in the valley alone. Alright?" He seems to think about it a moment before nodding his head.

"I want to argue, but I guess I don't have much of a choice here... I could call Jason or Tavish, but I'm not sure who will even hear the phone at this time of the morning on a Saturday..." I shake my head.

"No, please, you guys do enough. Honestly. I'll keep to the town where there's plenty of people around, I promise. I'll be fine."

He hesitates but nods his head and gets in the car.

"I'll come by tonight, okay? Either me or one of the boys. Just because this one is being a fucker, we aren't going to leave you on your own, all right?" I have no intention of making anyone else spend another night on my couch, but I nod so he's satisfied, and he pulls out of the parking lot.

My run hurts right away. My heart isn't in it. All it reminds me of with each step alone is that it's been months since I've been on my long run by myself. I wind through the downtown roads, stopping frustrated at each light, feeling my legs cramp up but too stubborn to be one of those people who jog in place at the intersection.

When I first got to college, I hated myself. I knew I had to change. Even with the people I met and the boys who asked me out on occasion, I heard Steve's voice in my head every moment, telling me I was ugly, that my body was soft and that the only reason anyone would want me was because I was easy. He would poke the places on me that jiggled, point out how no one else would want to see me naked, how lucky I was to have him since he was willing to put up with it. The last time I fought with him, he made more than clear that girls like me weren't the kind you took on your arm in public.

"I don't want to do this anymore. All you do is hurt me. I'm tired of pretending around Mom, too."

Steve laughed at me, his expression cruel, his eyes hard. *"Come on, Erika. You know I can't be seen out with you. I mean, I love your softness, you know that, but in public, I need someone like your mom. It's good for business, someone gorgeous and fit like she is. If I was with you, no one would hire me. They'd never believe I could make them look good."*

I look down at my body, the softness of my belly above my panties and the swell of my breasts over the cup of my bra.

"I told you I'd work out if you showed me how..."

Steve snorts, *"Nah, you should stay like this. Soft. I like it, you know that. I just can't be seen with it. Besides, girls like you don't change, not really. You'd work out for a week or maybe a month, but you'd go back to your ice cream and your couch, and all my work would be wasted anyways."*

I hate the tears when they come. "Why, then? Why do you want to be with me if I'm so fat and ugly?" He changes his expression to what he probably thinks is kindness, but it just looks fake, like a mask he puts on when he's lying.

"Oh, baby, you're not ugly. It's the world, the rest of the world thinks that. I'm the one with you, the one making you feel good..." He pauses, I think so I can agree, but I have no intention of doing that. It might have felt good for a few minutes in the beginning, when he would just touch me, but ever since I let him sleep with me, it only ever hurts. Thankfully, it's usually over quickly.

"That's why I care so much. That's why I can't let you leave me. No one else will be as understanding as I am..."

After that, he'd pinned me against the wall, running his hands up and down my sides a few times, whispering his backwards compliments before burying his face in my breasts. I closed my eyes so tight I saw stars, and I willed myself to be somewhere else as he led me to the ground. I let myself become pliable, what I know he wanted, moving to the position he's taught me is easiest for a 'big girl' like me as he took me roughly, dry, painfully. Like it had been every time since the first.

When he was done, he tossed my shirt at me and left without a word. I took a shower, crying on the floor until the water ran cold. The house was empty when I got out, and I packed up everything I needed from my room into a duffel bag and waited.

I think I knew. I knew that when Mom got home and I finally told her the truth, her teenage daughter's tearful confession of her stepfather's abuse, that she'd turn me away. I can't otherwise explain why I already had my bag packed except that I anticipated her hatred and the agonizing pain of her laughter at me when she told me the same thing Steve had. That no one would want me like I was, and that making up stories like that only made me seem desperate.

I got in the car and drove, pulling over when I couldn't see through the tears, I ended up sleeping on a side road in the driver's seat of my late-model Civic. When I got to my dad's in the late morning, I'd expected panic, but I should have known Mom had never even told him I had left. I never went back, not even when she divorced Steve for John.

When the old memories clear from my head, I look around and realize that I've long passed downtown. The suburban sprawl in front of me is unfamiliar, and my watch tells me I'm over thirty kilometers from my start point. With that realization, my legs make themselves known, reminding me that this was as far as I intended to go, no matter how far away my car is now. There's no way I'm making it the same distance back.

I turn around and walk to cool off, weighing my options. It would take me the rest of the day to walk back to where I left Bethany. I have my ID on me but nothing else, and I mentally chastise myself for ending up this far away with no cash and no transportation.

Eventually, I come across a convenience store where I ask

the bored-looking employee behind the counter if they'll call me a cab. I feel bad for not buying anything while I wait, but with nothing on me but a driver's license and a set of car keys, I don't have much choice. Thankfully, there's not a lot of requests for cabs at nine thirty on a Saturday morning, and it's not long before the yellow car pulls into the parking lot. It's still close to ten before I get to where I left Bethany and quickly grab my purse from the trunk, handing the driver my Visa. By now, I'm shivering, the sweat and heat from the run drying on my body and the chills setting in. Even though it's already almost twenty degrees, I crank the heat on the way home, skipping out on my usual breakfast stop and convincing myself it's not just because I don't have the desire to do it without Twiz with me. That only makes me angrier. I enjoyed that breakfast stop for years before I met him. Years. Somehow, in this short time, he's managed to take it from me.

I spend the day running errands and cleaning up around the house, busy work that seems empty. It's only been a matter of weeks since my routine changed to include Twiz but trying to go back to doing it all without him is harder than it should be. I told myself I wasn't getting attached, that our arrangement had always been temporary, that I don't need him around and that my heart didn't break at his words today. It's all a lie that doesn't even begin to work. By early evening, I'm curled up on my couch watching *Sweet Home Alabama* and eating sherbet when the doorbell rings.

Annoyed that Matt didn't even call before heading over so that I could have told him not to bother, I open the door, ready to let him know I'll be fine, and I'm instead greeted with a very pathetic-looking Twiz.

"Are you kidding me, Hellcat? You didn't even check to see who it was!"

"Well, you should be happy for it, you asshole. If I did, I never would have let you in!" I don't close the door on him like I probably should, however, and he takes the opening as permission to come inside. Closing it behind him, I turn around and walk back to the couch.

"Hel... Erika..." Twiz starts and the break in his voice has me turning around. "I'm sorry."

I take a good look at him. He's showered. I can tell because his hair is still a little damp, sticking up on top of his head. His eyes are red rimmed, and there's deep circles under them. His lips are chapped, his skin is pale, and he's just thrown on a pair of jeans and a t-shirt. They look like they came off the floor of his room, the deep creases in them almost comically rumpling his look.

"Are you even sober yet?"

It's been fourteen hours or so since we found him in the parking lot, but he'd been completely tanked. I've seen him drink plenty and I've never seen him stumble, fall over like that. I don't even know if he'd stopped drinking once Matt brought him home. He is standing upright, though, which is a better sign than the swaying he was doing this morning.

"Mostly," he admits sheepishly. "I didn't drive here. My truck is still in the parking lot at the river valley."

"And Matt let you leave the house?"

At this, he looks away.

"I don't answer to him." I just keep staring. I've had enough. "Fine. Matt was in the shower, okay?"

As if on cue, my phone rings. I look over at it, and then back at Twiz, who sighs and walks to the counter to pick it up.

"Yup." That's all he says as he answers it, and he's quiet for a moment, listening.

"I'm fine. I didn't drive. I came right here. The truck isn't... yes, I have the keys, but I'll wait. Yes. Yes. Look, ask her yourself." He holds the phone out in my direction. I take it, avoiding even letting my fingers brush his.

"Hey, Matt." I hear him take a deep breath and wonder what

he thought he might hear. Does he really think that Twiz would hurt me, or just that I would be devastated?

"Do you want me to come there and get him?" It's my turn for a deep breath. I have no idea what I want, but I'm sure that I can handle it myself.

"No, no. It's okay, Matt. I can deal with him."

He says nothing for a second and I can almost hear his thoughts. His sense of responsibility for Twiz, for all of them, must be so heavy some days. Especially days like today.

"Okay. Okay, but if you change your mind, call, okay? And if you throw him out..."

"I'll call. I promise."

He lets me go with a resigned sigh and I click the phone off, staring at it, refusing to look at the soldier in front of me for a long moment.

"Erika."

His voice is tortured, broken, and I finally look up. His eyes amaze me, the different ways the light hits the two colours. The brown looks dark, hurt, while the blue looks sharp and cold. It makes him that much harder to read.

It's not hard to read the pain, though, when he leans his back against the door behind him and lets himself slide to the floor.

"I fucked up, Hellcat."

"Ya. You did."

I say nothing else, just walk to the kitchen, grabbing a half-full bottle of cheap chardonnay, pouring myself a glass. I grab a bottle of water from the fridge and place it on the floor next to him, sitting across from him cross legged.

"Why?"

"Because I can't keep you, Hellcat. I've had too much fun, playing house with you, but it's not fair. You will have the chance to find a nice guy one day and if I'm here fucking around, you won't get the opportunity."

159

I swallow down the hurt that sits on my chest at his rejection of anything real.

"You aren't making any sense. Besides, what makes you think I want more than this? Maybe this is all I want?"

He looks up at me with the saddest expression, the smallest, pathetic smile on his lips, and I read hope in his eyes.

"Nah. It's not. You deserve more."

I stand. I'm getting tired of being told what I want.

"So, be more."

He drops his head again and shakes it.

"I can't. You don't understand. I just... it's not safe. I can't. Ever."

"Then explain it to me if I don't understand, Twiz! Because it makes no sense!"

He doesn't explain. Instead, he just stands, swaying just a little. He puts his flat palm against the wall behind him for a moment for balance before putting his hand down to lift me until I'm standing nose to nose in front of him.

"They kicked me out of my platoon."

"I got that. You know, this morning. When you called me a whore and accused me of sleeping with the friend that you sent here."

I want to turn my back and walk away, but I stay right where I am, where I can feel the mint of his freshly brushed teeth. I won't give him an out, a way to avoid looking me in the eye and explaining what he did.

"You fucking hurt me, Twiz."

I can tell he wants to run. I feel his muscles twitch and the movement of his jaw where he's biting his tongue between his front teeth like he does.

"That's what I do, Erika. It's probably best that it happened now, like this, instead of something worse later."

This time it's my turn to shake my head.

"Why do you act like it's guaranteed you'll hurt me? You have a choice, Twiz. Just don't."

"It's not that easy, okay! It's who I am!" Now his breath comes in soft pants in front of me, but we still both hold our ground.

"That's bullshit."

We're not getting anywhere, so I am the one who finally breaks our connection, placing my glass gently in the sink before walking to the closet, grabbing a pillow and blanket and throwing it at him where he's still standing transfixed in the kitchen.

"You're still too drunk to drive. Get some sleep. I'm tired." He doesn't move to grab the bedding, and it falls to the ground in front of him. When he looks up from the bundle on the floor, the conflict in his eyes isn't hidden at all. I know he wants me. He just has to figure out what he's willing to do about it.

Just when I think he might give in and step over it all and follow me to bed, he drops down and grabs it, toeing off his shoes and heading to the couch.

"Good night, Hellcat."

19

TWIZ

I'm ashamed at how fast I fall asleep but considering other than a couple of quick blackouts last night and this morning, I haven't slept since yesterday, I guess I'm not surprised.

I hadn't really thought through my trip here. Grabbing my keys and wallet and closing the door quietly behind me to the cab, I was only thinking I needed to get out quick before Matt stopped me. I know he had no intention on letting me see Erika again, not after what he heard me say.

To be honest, I didn't have a lot of intention of seeing her again, either. I just knew that once I was a little cleaner and marginally more sober, I didn't want anyone else there with her tonight keeping her safe. My brain only has room for about two thoughts in my head at that point and wanting to be with her and not wanting to be with her made up those two.

I knew she wouldn't want to see me. I didn't even think she'd let me in. All I could think when she did, however, was how easily I could have been someone else, and how my chest physically hurts at the idea of her being hurt.

What's the point of keeping her safe from me if I let her be hurt by someone else like me?

As soon as I lie my head on her pillow, smelling the scent of her laundry soap and just that smell that her home has, I am immediately out. It's not until I am jolted up that I realize something's wrong. At first, I think it's just a nightmare, or another panic attack, but it's not.

Someone's trying to get in her door. I can hear the jiggling of the handle, and then the scrape of a key. I glance at the stove that says it's after three a.m.

I move silently, thankful that sleep has removed even the last bit of alcohol from my system, grateful for the silence that years of working with my rifle has brought me. For just a half moment, I take the chance to enjoy her prone frame, asleep in her shorts and tank top, oblivious to the noise I can hear at the door, the soft click of it opening, and a footstep inside.

Erika opens her eyes as soon as I step closer, and I'm grateful for the awareness she seems to have of what's around her. She doesn't panic when she sees me, just takes a moment to blink and then watches me, waiting for instructions.

I grab the phone on her nightstand and dial 911, whispering, "Send help, police" as quietly but clearly as I can and then leaving it open without speaking, but not shutting it off, either. I'm hoping the dispatcher can hear the shuffling and any altercation and get the idea to send the cops sooner than later.

Then I pull Erika up as silently as I can and move her to the closet, tucking her in the back while I stand in the front, so grateful that I'm in my clothes and not the usual nothing that I've been in other nights I've stayed here.

I can hear the soft padding of the footprints in her apartment. Whoever is inside isn't very good at hiding their approach. This bodes well for me. They're clearly not professionals. This helps, because I'm barely awake and don't even have a weapon on me.

I walk slowly, deliberately to the other side of the doorframe and wait. It seems to take forever, which is funny because I've waited for days for a target. Staring at the closet that holds Erika, though, knowing she's here, that I'm responsible for her safety, that's more than any of the rest of the times I've had to make these calls. Usually, the people with me are just as capable and trained as I am.

I'm not sure what he's doing out there, but it's taking some time, and close to ten minutes pass that I count over in my head before I hear the footsteps close in on the bedroom.

When the door finally opens with a soft click, I press my back against the wall and wait.

There's a moment of confusion I can actually hear from the assailant when they realize that the bed is empty, and I mentally kick myself for not propping the sheets to give the impression she's still in it.

I will my breath down, however, since I still haven't been seen, and the sound of it is almost silent even to me. Years of training kick in. My eyes have already adjusted to the dark, which gives me the advantage over the intruder and I can see that Steve, Ericka's ex-stepfather and ex-lover, is not Steve at all.

Unless Steve is a woman.

A woman with a big ass knife in her hand.

I count three breaths, in and out, after that realization when there is a loud, insistent knock on the door.

"Edmonton Police! Open up!"

Not-Steve turns abruptly and I use the momentum to grab them from behind, the arm that held a knife twists as the shiny object hits the floor and I hit their back with my knee, bringing them down to the floor with a thud.

Erika bolts past us to the front door, and I hear a couple of officers coming inside. Her breathless explanations I barely process as I kneel with my knee on this stranger's back in the dark, catching my breath.

Finally looking down, the first thing I realize is my captive is small. Tall, but thin and boney, almost frail, and I shift my weight to take some of it off her spine.

Her.

She's a redhead, but the colour looks bottled, not like Erika's. It's all different shades and curled at the bottom, like you would expect to see on a commercial for a hair salon or something. It strikes me funny, kneeling here holding this knife-wielding intruder down, that they obviously styled their hair before coming on this break-and-enter mission.

I look up as the profile of two uniformed police officers enters the doorway, standing momentarily as shadows from the light of the hall until one flicks on the light in the room. I nod my head to a knife laying on the ground where it fell, and the one officer kicks it further away before the other comes over to me, taking my spot and allowing me to get up before hauling the intruder onto her feet.

Up until now, she's said nothing, and it all happened so fast in the dark, I hadn't thought much about why. Until I hear Erika's voice barely above a whisper from behind me.

"Mom?"

Oh. Shit.

The intruder, Erika's MOM, raises her head finally from where she's kept it bent and looks at her daughter with the kind of hate I've only ever seen in the eyes of terrorists. Usually, right before I shot them.

"Mom?" she taunts, repeating the question with a high-pitched and whiny voice before breaking out and laughing. "Oh please, cut the innocent act."

"Look how surprised your little boy toy is that it's me, though. I bet he wasn't thinking he was pressing himself up against your mother... I mean, why would he? I barely look old enough..."

Is she serious? I look around the room dumbstruck, almost expecting cameras. There's no way this woman is real life. Is she *hitting* on me?

The officers in the room look completely confused by this family drama, stunned for a moment. One holds Erika's mom with her arms behind her back, putting cuffs on, and the other talks quietly in his radio.

"I'm going to need a statement..." the one doing the cuffing speaks up, turning her towards the door but Erika finally finds her voice.

"What the fuck, Mom? I don't understand. Where's Steve?"

"Who fucking cares, Erika?!? You already poisoned him. Now I'm getting married again and I can't let you stick around to ruin that too, now can I?" She looks around to the police officers that are both watching her. "She sleeps with her stepfathers. How am I supposed to stay married when she sleeps with my husbands?"

At this, the cop holding his radio just stops, mouth open, and stares.

"I thought Steve..." I move to stand with Erika and gently touch my hand to hers, and she instantly grabs on tightly.

"You thought Steve... of course you did! You just assumed you were *so amazing* that my ex-husband would just keep stalking you. Well, you're not that fucking great, Erika!"

With that, the officer takes her out of the room, and Erika just looks at me, the hurt in her pouring out in every blink of her confusion.

"My name is Constable Parkinson. We responded to a 911 call to this location. Did you make that call?"

I look at him for the first time. He's taller than I am, putting him quite a bit over six feet. He's leaner, though, with dirty-blond hair cut close to his head military style. His face is scarred with what would look like some serious chickenpox marks, if I hadn't seen similar ones before. I would guess those are shrapnel injuries.

"That was me. I was sleeping on the couch, and I heard the person at the door. I went to Erika and called 911 from here. The phone is right there. I never hung up with the dispatcher." I gesture over to the phone and the Constable picks it up and puts it to his ear.

"Constable Parkinson. Oh, hi Patty. Yup, we've got it. Thanks." He presses the button to hang up.

"How did they get in? Does this person have a key?" Erika shakes her head.

"No, no, she shouldn't. Unless my dad gave her his, I guess. I don't know how she got in."

"The person definitely had some kind of key. That's the sound I woke up to."

He keeps writing in his notepad, and I wrap Erika up against my chest. She's shivering, and I kick myself for not remembering she's in just a tank top and tiny little shorts. I grab the comforter off her bed and wrap it around her shoulders. It says a lot about her state of mind that she hasn't noticed, either. She almost folds herself into the blanket once it's on her, though, and despite the crazy situation and the fear for our lives, I still pull it all the way around to cover the way her nipples push against her tank top. I'm a bastard, and I don't want them all looking at her.

"I take it you know this person, though?"

Erika shudders even with the extra layer around her.

"She's my mother. I haven't seen her in years, though. Haven't even spoken to her. I thought she was Steve."

"Who's Steve, ma'am?"

"Steve was, well, he was my stepdad. She's right. He and I had a relationship when I was in my teens."

"You were how old?" He looks up with compassion, his pen

stilling on the pad of paper. "Because there's no statute of limitations for child abuse, and I'd be required to report that, ma'am."

"No, no. I wasn't a child. Late teens. It's not... Anyways, I ended it quickly. It didn't last long. But he kept bugging me after. I just assumed when I kept getting the notes and the phone messages and the spray paint... I just assumed it was..." She fades off, staring out at nothing, and I give her that moment to think.

"Erika has recently filled out a police report regarding harassment, including spray paint on her door. She was given the forms for a restraining order against Steve. Since he had previously been the one harassing her, she believed this was just an escalation of his behavior. We just went in to file it earlier this week." The officer continues to write furiously in his notebook, and we wait a moment. We can hear with our silence the conversation just outside the door where the other constable must be with Erika's mom.

"It's not break and enter if I had a damn key! I'm her mother!" I can't hear what the cop is saying since he's speaking to her softly, probably attempting to de-escalate her, but I can hear all her responses.

"Her damn boyfriend wasn't even supposed to be here. His truck isn't parked outside... I just wanted to talk to my daughter. She hasn't returned my calls."

With that, Erika scoffs. I point back over to the knife.

"That fell out of her hand when I grabbed her. I didn't touch it."

"It's mine, though." Erika sighs. "She must have taken it from my kitchen."

"That's okay." The officer pulls on a pair of gloves and grabs the knife, putting it in a bag. "We will still take it. Might have prints on it of hers so we can at least prove she grabbed it. She's not wearing gloves. Do you know why she'd want to hurt you?"

Any idea why she broke in here tonight?"

"Nothing more than what she's already said. I mean, this whole time I thought it was just Steve. I never considered it would be her, I don't even know now what she did and what he did! The notes on my car, the spray paint on the door, the emails and phone calls... I don't know now!" She throws her hands up and sits on the edge of the bed. I sit next to her.

"It's okay, Hellcat. We've got her, it's okay."

There's a few more voices from the front of her condo, and the other officer from before pokes his head in the bedroom.

"Backup came, and they have the individual in the car outside. I know you've answered a lot of questions, but could you come out here with us for a while and answer just a few more so we can get this all settled?"

Erika just nods, and I follow her back to the kitchen.

IT'S WELL INTO MORNING. The sun is already all the way up before all the police officers have gone. Statements have been made and Erika's mom, who it turns out is named Carly, leaves in the back of a car. The officers are pretty sure she won't be locked up for long this time, but they'll try to keep her considering the risk she obviously poses to Erika. She's not saying much, but it sounds like she's getting married quickly and has been harbouring serious hatred for her daughter. She's convinced Erika was the reason she can't keep a husband. She's sure that she had to 'talk" to her tonight to keep her away from this new one. Turns out, Erika has never even laid eyes on him, but it sounds like he's my age.

Erika sits at the kitchen island with an empty cup of coffee in her hands. It's the same empty cup she's been holding since she finished it a half hour ago. I walk over and take it from her, placing it on the counter and wrapping her up in my arms.

"Do you think she would have really hurt me?" she asks in a

tiny voice that makes me even angrier with that woman who makes Erika feel small. No one should make her feel small.

"I don't know. But it's over now. It's over, and you're safe. I'm so sorry this happened, but I'm so glad I was here."

"Oh, God, what if you hadn't come over??" She starts to shake, and I hold on tighter.

"I did, though, Hellcat. I did come over, and I was here. Now it's over and you're safe."

There's a long period where we just stand like that in the kitchen until there's a soft knock on the door. It opens, and Erika's dad stares at us.

"Carly called her new fiancé, but he won't bail her out. He called me. I don't even know how he got my number, but he called me to let me know what happened. He's leaving her."

Erika nods and sniffles, and I grab a napkin with my free hand and delicately wipe her cheeks. "This will just be another reason for her to hate me, I guess."

"Oh, baby, none of this was your fault." Stewart looks gutted, and I know what I must do. I move slowly, so I don't even think she notices we're moving at all, until we're right next to her dad. Then I shift, just a little, until it's his shoulder she's leaning on, and I'm the one standing on my own. She collapses in sobs on her father's chest, and I take just a quick glance back at her gorgeous red hair under her father's hand before I softly click the door behind me.

She doesn't need me anymore, so now's the time to walk away.

2 0

ERIKA

*T*wiz probably thought when he left, he would slip out without me noticing, but I did.

I can still hear the door clicking, even weeks later.

It's funny, how life goes on even when you feel like everything has changed.

Dad was amazing. I didn't realize he would have it in him. Even in the time that followed, with the statements and court, he had my back. Thankfully, Mom decided to plead guilty to criminal harassment for spray painting the door and coming in the house while I was sleeping. She admitted to some of the phone calls, too, and realizing that the stalking and harassment was her changed everything... Turns out she saw it start with the phone calls and in person from Steve right before they divorced, but when he was gone right after, she kept it up, trying to scare me from stealing any more of her husbands. She really is delusional.

When I finally get contacted by the person I gave the no-contact order to, they tell me they finally did track him down. To a motorcycle accident in Pattaya, Thailand, where he was killed five years ago.

That means that once him and Mom divorced the rest of the harassment could never have been him, and knowing all those violent, hurtful messages came from my mom is harder than I thought it would be to process.

I dropped the charges of break and enter and attempted assault with a weapon since with the key, it was hard to prove. Honestly, I just wanted it over with. Especially when she said she would take her sentence of probation and restraining order and move to BC to some treatment facility slash commune. That sounds about right. I just wanted her gone.

The guys all showed up at court for sentencing. Even Twiz. He didn't say anything to me, though, and because she put in a guilty plea, there was no fanfare. Just handing out her consequences, move on to the next case. I didn't even hear a gavel like in the movies. It was more like an office meeting. They were gone by the time I was out the door, with only Jason giving me a small wave as they climbed into Twiz's truck outside.

I didn't say a word to Mom, either, when she was led back out. Just stared. I stared at the overdyed hair, compensating I'm sure for the grey that must be creeping in now. She'd spent the while before at the Remand Center, so she was dressed simply in slacks and a shirt, without the layers of makeup and jewelry. She looked far closer to the fifty-three she was instead of the twenty-five she perpetually tried to be. Instead of this gorgeous, looming monster, she just looked like a sad woman, desperate for attention.

Which made me realize that more than anything, I didn't want to be her. Ever.

I never would have thought I was. I mean, I had never been married or even come close. Never had surgery. I never would have even put us in the same category.

Except my spotless apartment overlooking the river. The fitness classes far above and beyond healthy and bordering on obsession, the fact that even when it should be a rest day, I can't seem to stay home. The mornings in front of the mirror, pulling at all the right places to remind myself how much work I had to do. The lists in my head, of all I can control physically to look a certain way. The calorie counting.

The string of men in my bed, not always because it was a good time but more times than I would like to admit, because I needed them to want me, so I would feel like I had worth.

I may not be a serial bride, but I was slipping to a place where I could almost see how she got there.

And that's terrifying.

Dad makes me take a few weeks off work, which only makes things worse. I'm going stir crazy in the house. With Thanksgiving coming up, I decide I need to do something. Next on my list of leaving my bubble of control is friends, and that starts with a phone call.

Jordyn is doing so well in her new place with Jeremy. Jules has almost finished with her training, and school is finally all done for her. She has a shiny degree that will always be a little spoiled for her, and she moved right away to full time work at the pub instead. Her eyes are still haunted but there's a pep in her walk and a blush on her cheeks every time Jeremy's name comes up, which is often.

And interesting.

I sit with her for a few minutes in a coffee shop just down the street from the pub. I offered to meet her there, but she understandably was looking for a reason to get away from the building she both works and lives in.

"I'm sorry I couldn't do more with all that happened," she says, taking a sip from her chai tea and grimacing at the heat, putting it back down quickly.

"Nothing to be sorry for, Jordyn. You had your own shit going on, and anyways, I was fine. Twiz was there when it happened, and the rest was just paperwork and moping at home with ice cream..."

"That sounds like my kind of thing." She gives a shy smile.

"Well, good. I'm hoping you and Beth and Juliette and the boys will come over to my place for Thanksgiving in a couple of weeks."

The smile that takes over her face is amazing, and I'm even happier about my plan when I see it.

"Really?"

"Ya, really." Right on cue, Jules and Tavish come, and he pulls a chair out for her before plopping down across the table. Beth and Jason skirt in, too, and there seems to be more distance between them than usual. I remind myself for not the first time that they're roommates, not a couple. According to my calls last week, Matt is away somewhere, and Twiz has never returned a single message I've sent.

And I've sent an embarrassing amount. I'm done, and the ball's in his court.

"Thanksgiving??" Juliette doesn't skip an excited beat. "Can we really do Thanksgiving? I can't cook, really... I can bring wine!" Tavish laughs at her.

"No, you can't cook. I can bring something, but wine is probably your best bet though." She kicks him under the table and he smirks at her.

"You said it first!"

"You should have defended me!"

"Baby, no one will defend your last attempt at a turkey." He looks over to me and puts his hand to the side to pretend as though Jules can't see. He widens his eyes and shakes his head violently, mouthing, "It was the worst."

I laugh. The rest of the table groans.

"We don't do holiday meals at Cleary's unless they're ordering in from now on," Jason says, and Juliette makes an exaggerated pout.

"No one is bringing anything, except maybe alcohol. I guess I can take that. I'm going to make the dinner. I'm going stir crazy at home and I still owe the boys for..."

Tavish cuts me off, "...for nothing. You don't owe us for anything. We don't need a reason to show up for dinner. Juliette and I are in! I'm excited for good food!" The swat she gives him is only half-hearted.

"I'm in too," Beth says, and Jason nods along with her.

Jordyn speaks up next. "I already said I'm in, and I'll make grumpy come, too."

"Good, then! It's settled. We'll eat Saturday, if that's okay for everyone. Maybe at my place around noon, and we can go from there?" They all nod, and conversation moves on to work for Jules and Jordyn, some new part Tavish added to his motorcycle, and Beth's promotion.

As it filters to some of the topics more on the farther end of the table, Tavish takes the moment to lean over to me.

"He's doing okay."

I nod, not having to ask who he's talking about.

"We won't let him disappear, and he's been going to his appointments. He's going to need time."

"I'm glad he's doing okay." I try to say nonchalant, as though it doesn't kill me not to be there for him. Tavish doesn't come close to believing my mask, but he doesn't call me out on it, either.

"I wish I could say he'll come to this with us..."

"It's fine, honestly. We had a good run, but it was time to move on. Not a big deal. He's welcome to come. Or not. It's fine." Ya, Erika, how about you say the word fine again.

Seriously.

Tavish believes the rambling about as much as I do, but he still doesn't say anything, just nods at me. Soon, it's time for Jules and Jordyn to get back to work, and Jason and Tavish have some kind of guy-date I'm not going to ask too much about. Just as we all get to the parking lot, though, Jules turns around.

"Let's have a wine night!" she says triumphantly, as though she's just come up with the solution to everything.

"Um... sure?"

"No, really. Beth and Jordyn and me and you. We'll bring the wine to your place. Just like we did with Megan." Beth nods to her, and I just stare since I have no idea what she's going on about, but a night with the girls would be a good step towards my new plan of having friends.

"Okay, sure. You mean tonight?"

"Why not? Let's do it. We're done at the pub at eight. The staff can take it from there to close. It's about time. I'll get Tavish to drop us off."

"You will, hey?" he says with no anger in his voice, only amusement.

"Mhmm." She smiles and kisses him, and I have to look away. Dammit, why does this all make me jealous? I never missed having a guy around before. They've always been just an accessory, not a requirement.

Now I miss Twiz's smell and the way he could shadow my runs. I miss being called Hellcat, even though I never understood why. I miss his eyes and how I could flit between the two of them to see different emotions. I miss how easy it became to fall asleep next to him.

Also, I hate that I miss him.

I'm quick to get home, grabbing some snacks and lighting a few candles before the doorbell rings a few hours later. The girls stand on the other side and an amused Tavish behind them.

"You sticking around, Slick?" Juliette asks, but he shakes his head.

"Just walking you up. Give me a call when you're ready to get picked up. Jason or I will come getcha. Don't leave the apartment until we're at the door." His voice is stern as he looks down at her, and she mock salutes.

"Yessir, Master Corporal Cleary, sir." She giggles, and he rolls his eyes.

"Not a sir. Don't be a smartass." He smacks her butt as she walks in and he gives me a smile and heads back out. I notice that he twists the doorknob to lock it behind him.

"Woohoo, girls' night!" Juliette whoops and I giggle.

"Sorry," she says a little sheepishly. "I don't get out much. And I never really had girlfriends when I was younger, so I have to make up for all that now."

"Me neither," says Jordyn, and I agree too. Beth giggles at us. "I did, I guess. Not like this, though."

We settle on the couches once I've poured the wine for everyone.

"So, how did you two meet?" I motion to Juliette and Beth, and they look at each other a moment. Something flashes between them, and Beth speaks up first.

"I knew Juliette before I met her. Tavish carried her with him."

At this, Jules makes this gagging noise before laughing, but her shit-eating smile gives her away.

"Tavish and I met in high school, but we didn't get together until 2006. I saw him in Calgary, and I ended up moving into his apartment before they all went to Afghanistan. I met Beth right before they left, and we hung out a ton while they were gone."

"I wouldn't have made it through Silas' death without her," Beth says, but it's with a contented smile. There's pain there, but there's a lot of acceptance that I don't know that I understand yet.

"I remember when that happened. Megan and I were friends, and she left for Calgary..."

"Ya, the funeral was there. Honestly, Jules did everything for me. She was amazing. She moved in with me after that, too, and then Jason moved in when he ended up coming home."

There's something amazing about it, this friendship built on that kind of loss. I feel like an outsider for a moment before I remember Jordyn is here by the sound of her sniffles.

"That's so beautiful," she whispers.

"Who's Silas?"

"Silas was my fiancé. He was killed in Afghanistan. Tavish brought him home."

With that, Jordyn only sniffles more, but Beth simply hands her a tissue.

"No more of that, or you'll get us going. It's been a few years now, and I'm okay. I miss him, every day, so much, but I'm okay. That's been a big step, admitting that I'm okay even when he's gone."

Juliette smiles and squeezes her knee, and then one of them asks Jordyn about work and the conversation moves on.

Later in the evening, two plates of munchies and several bottles of wine later, Juliette turns to me with a determined look on her face.

"So, Twiz..."

I swallow hard. I knew this would come up, but I'm still not ready. Jordyn pipes up.

"I haven't seen him around!" she says cheerfully, probably completely unaware of how things are or what went down.

"Me neither." I shrug, as though it's no big deal.

"I have," Jules says softer this time.

"He looks... Lost."

My heart physically hurts at her words, but I try not to plaster the pain all over my face.

"I'm glad he's got his friends with him for this."

Jordyn pipes up, looking confused. "I don't mean to pry, but is he okay?"

"He will be," I assure her, and I'm sure of my words as I say them. He's strong. "He's just been struggling with work stuff lately. All my stress probably didn't help either..."

"No, don't do that. Twiz doesn't do shit he doesn't want to. He was there for you because he cares about you."

I take a deep breath. It's time to jump into this whole friend thing.

"I miss him. I told him no strings and I'll honour that, even if I wish now I could change it. I think maybe all that with my mom and learning about the kind of person I am..."

"Bullshit." Juliette sits up a little on the couch and stares at me. "Bullshit, Erika. Twiz wouldn't care about that and besides, no part of it was your fault. He just has his own... issues. Trust me, it's not you."

"So, it's not me, it's him?"

"Exactly. He'll get his head out of his ass eventually. Until then, you do you."

"I'm trying to be me. Or at least, learn who she can be and then be her."

Jules smiles wide. "I had to do that. I did it without Tavish, too. I don't think it would have been the same if I hadn't had that time without him to be me first. Maybe there's a reason for all this."

I take a moment to let that sink in. "Well, one thing on my list was making friends, even though friends do things like get cancer and almost die and then move away..." I cover my mouth with my hand. I don't even know where that came from.

"Oh, Erika," Jules says, and cocks her head to the side. Beth takes the moment to speak up.

"And fiancé's die and people get hurt or break down or move out or get sick or run away... People can't be controlled, Erika. Having the right friends, the right people in your life, though, is worth it."

"I've never had girlfriends before, either. So, I guess we're both growing!" Jordyn interjects and smiles big and we all laugh.

"Hells ya, we are!"

It feels good, and our conversation moves to Jordyn's plans in the coming year and the possibility of one day seeing little Clearys running around. Which we are all sold on because those would be cute babies.

I want to bug Jordyn about Jeremy but so many times I open my mouth and then close it. I'm not sure she's at a place yet where she can joke about a guy's affections, and I don't want to make her first real girls' night anything other than amazing. She looks so happy, just being around everyone.

Eventually, Beth yawns and Jules steps to the kitchen to give Tavish a call. As she gets up, Beth grabs her arm but then doesn't say anything when Jules looks down at her. She gives a questioning look before she seems to figure it out, and she just gives a sad smile.

"I'll be sure that Slick drives."

When she's gone, Beth just lets out a long breath before I catch her eye.

"I just worry," she says dismissively. "Jason takes his meds at night."

It's not the whole story so I just wait.

"He's taking too much still." She sighs. "I know he is, and I know he's getting them from somewhere, too. They're not all from his prescription anymore. I'm not sure what to do, but I'm going to figure it out."

I'm amazed at her strength, at both of them.

"If there's anything I can do…"

"I'm sure when the time comes, it will take all of us. Just not sure it's there, yet."

I nod, and the warmth of being included in the us washes over me. When Juliette comes back in the room, we have another fifteen minutes of laughter before there's a knock at the door.

Jules pounds back what's left in her red wine glass as she answers to her husband.

"Really, Jules?"

"It's only my third glass! I don't want it to go to waste!" He shakes his head but grins. Leaning down, he pushes his shoulder into her torso and lifts her off the ground and over his shoulder. She wiggles her tiny little butt in the air in her painted-on jeans, Tavish reaches down to grab her heels from the floor with his other arm.

"I don't mind, baby. I'll get lucky tonight!"

"You *always* get lucky," she mumbles into his back.

"What's that?" he asks, and she looks at me conspiratorial.

"I love you!"

He just snorts.

"You want the same treatment, girls? I bet I can carry you both!" Jason's imposing shadow enters my doorway. Jordyn blushes, and Beth just scoffs.

"Don't even think about it, Jay." She pulls her shoes on and with a quick kiss goodbye to me, brushes past him to the hallway. Jordyn squeaks goodbye and scurries like a mouse after her. Once she's gone, Jason grimaces.

"Shit. I hope I didn't…"

"You're okay," I assure him. "She's stronger than she looks. It's just going to take her a while. Or not. Let's let her decide."

He nods and heads out, with Tavish and a still squirming Jules right behind him. By the time I close the door, I feel like I've done something different.

I've made real friends.

If only for all my positive steps, I didn't feel like I was always still missing a piece.

21

TWIZ

*J*t takes weeks, but when I walk out of the mental health office this time, I feel slightly less like throwing up.

The first time I went, I had to call Matt from the parking lot. I was sure that was a huge step backwards, but my social worker informs me it was amazing because I agreed to let him help me.

Truth is I just didn't have another choice, but I'll take the win.

After that, I always had a ride there and back. Sometimes a silent one while I processed, sometimes one where I got my ass handed to me for not putting the work in, sometimes which ever guy picked me up would just stop in an empty lot for a bit and let me rage. Once, Tav had to pull over while I lost my breakfast on the side of the highway. Matt brought me butter chicken while I plastered and painted the hole I'd put in the wall one night, though he didn't help me fix it since that's how I learn. I woke up the morning after a particularly hard session humiliated when I realized I was sleeping on the phone I'd used to call Jason when I couldn't make the panic stop, only to see him fast asleep on the chair in the corner.

No one has ever complained, though, or even said a word about what's happening. They're just... there.

I've never been more grateful for the family I have been given.

I thought I'd hate being behind a desk, but in truth, I'm enjoying working on training, and the upstairs office gives me a chance to avoid them all when I need it.

Watching Matt go in the field this past couple weeks on training without me, that part hurt. I know they were all worried. Tavish and Jason have been at our place almost every night while Matt's gone, and while I complain every single moment about feeding and entertaining them, I'm grateful I haven't had the chance to fall back into a bottle.

Even when Jason puts his feet on my coffee table and Tavish eats enough for five of us.

I wanted to say that it would be a few weeks, a few sessions, and I'd be back to normal and good to go.

I can't.

The best I have right now is the ability to admit that.

I can do that. I can admit it's not back to the way it was, but mostly because I try hard not to think about it.

Which is working better than the effort I'm putting into not thinking about Erika.

I might be letting go of my career, which up until this year, would have been the worst thing that could have happened to me.

Letting go of Erika, though?

It might be harder.

I know the guys have seen her. She has left me messages in the first couple of weeks. Like the coward I am, I have never even listened to them. I know they would have broken me down. Instead, I just flat-out ignore everything to do with her, which is getting harder and harder. She's there every time I close my eyes.

I go out, twisting my counsellor's words about 'getting out to meet people' to mean I should find a woman for a night like I used to, but as I sit at the bar chatting up the drop-dead gorgeous blonde, because I can't bring myself to find a redhead, I can't do it.

Even after a couple of drinks. Even once the music gets louder and she sways her hips while she stands between my open legs as I sit at the barstool, I can't.

Instead, I pay for her drink, shuffle her back over to where her friends sit, give her a kiss on the cheek, and put myself in one of the waiting cabs outside the front doors of the bar.

My counsellor tells me the next week that meeting people will get easier with time. She doesn't know why I left Erika, though. No one does. She's only supposed to help with my post-traumatic stress from the deployment, not my love life or what-ever demons lurk from my childhood, so it doesn't seem that important anyways.

Maybe life without her won't get better.

I probably deserve that.

Instead, the counsellor and I talk about Afghanistan. It takes three appointments for us to even get to this last deployment. I manage to talk about everything but for far longer than I should have, but her patience is pretty impressive, and she doesn't give up. Once I get to the girl, and the shot, and the rifle, and the blood, she's not even a little surprised.

Somehow, this means I keep talking.

I even go to her peer support group. We're working up to maybe one day saying something there, but we'll see.

Today, there is a prescription.

It takes me this long, back and forth, for her to suggest and me to admit that I think this might work at controlling the panic attacks. Or at the very least, can't make it worse. So, she writes something on a pad of paper that I take to the pharmacy on base where the guy behind the counter doesn't even blink.

He hands them over a few minutes later with some explanation on how to take them and when, and I walk out feeling like I have a thousand-pound weight in my pocket instead of a few ounces of pills.

When I get home, I put them on the coffee table, in the middle of the room, and stare at them. I turn on the TV, but I keep looking over at the bottle every couple of minutes like it might detonate. When the door opens to a dirty Matt who smells like the lack of shower I know he's not had, I don't move them.

He only nods at me and it's less than a minute before I hear the shower running, and the thud of his combats on top of the washer. I don't blame him. It's hard to think of much else but a hot shower and clean clothes when you get home from that long out in the field.

By the time he makes it back to the living room, with a pair of clean sweats and a t-shirt on and his hair still damp, I've served up some of the leftover chicken I made earlier in the week and turned on the History Channel. He plops unceremoniously onto the couch and digs in while we watch black and white footage of Vietnam.

It took a few days after he picked me up downtown with Erika for us to say anything to each other. Work, home, we both just functioned on autopilot and didn't acknowledge the other until finally by the middle of that next week, I caught him in the kitchen before bed and said, "I'm an asshole."

"Yup." He didn't even take his head out of where it was in the fridge, scrounging a snack.

"Sorry."

With that, he does look, closing the fridge door and popping the top of a can of Coke.

"I won't put up with the drunk-driving shit, Twiz."

"I know."

"And I won't let you talk like that to Erika."

"I know."

He looks up and glares.

"I apologized to her. I'm not seeing her anymore, so it won't be a problem."

He just shook his head at me after that and that was it. Life went on and we didn't bring it up again.

Eventually, as we watch TV, his eyes drift to the coffee table and I see them catch the bottle that I've left there. Which seems like the easiest way to have this conversation.

"Those helping?" he asks. First words since I've seen him.

"I haven't taken them yet." He just nods and goes back to watching.

"What's stopping you?"

I think about that for a minute.

"I just got them today. And I don't know."

"That shit in your head is just like anything else. If they gave you something for your bad knee or an ulcer or something, you'd take that right away. I fucking gobbled the ibuprofen the medics gave me in the field. So, why not this?"

"You don't have to be so fucking logical all the time, you know." I shake my head, but I grab the bottle and shake a little white pill into my hand.

"No one thinks less of you, Rob." I look up at my real name. No one ever uses it, and I know he's only pulling it out to make a point. I toss it back with my bottle of water.

"Here's hoping."

He nods, and we go back to watching the show without another word. Which is how we manage to stay friends. We talk, especially when it's important. But no more than we have to.

It's perfect.

After a while, he gets up, slapping my knee.

"Let's go to the pub." I jump up but then stop.

"I don't think I should drink on those pills."

"Excellent, you're driving." He grabs my truck keys from beside the door and throws them at me and we head out. Predictably, Tavish and Juliette, and Jason and Beth are sitting in a booth at the back. Matt slides in and I pull up a chair at the end.

"Look who's back!" Jason says, and Matt nods at everyone, giving Jules and Beth a little kiss on the cheek each. "How was the field?"

"Cold. Dirty. Long." He shrugs, and we all grunt in agreement. That's the best way to describe it most times.

The three of them start up with the work talk. I join in once in a while. It feels strange, though, like I'm on the outside even though I'm not. I work in the same area as Matt at battalion. I see a lot of the guys every single day.

I won't be deploying back to Afghanistan, or anywhere else anytime soon though. Maybe never.

It hurts and it's also a relief, and I haven't figured out what that feels like together yet.

"Hey, we're missing Erika," Jordyn says as she comes over to bring our drinks. I freeze and predictably, everyone looks at me.

"Don't keep her away on my account, guys. I'm a big boy. I don't need to avoid someone just because we stopped sleeping together."

"Oh, fuck off!" Jordyn says and then slaps a hand over her mouth. Everyone's eyes at the table widen before they all laugh.

"I'm so sorry."

"You have no reason to be sorry, baby girl. But... huh?"

"It's just that you work so hard at pretending that all you guys did was have sex when that's such a load of crap, and everyone knows it." I look around the table to nodding heads.

"It's not going to happen, guys. You knew this about me when you met me. Erika's great. It's not her, it's me."

"We know that. We told her the same thing."

"Well, thanks? I think?"

"You know, Twiz, as much as you guys think you can do anything, you can't just stop yourself from falling in love." This time it's Juliette, and I'd be mad, but she just looks so compassionate when she says it. I can't bring myself to tell her off.

Either that, or it's her big-ass husband sitting between us.

I brush it off, instead.

"Ya, maybe you all underestimate what I can do..." No one buys it. They just all give up, going back to their conversations. After a few more minutes, I decide to head outside. Even though I quit smoking years ago, I never stopped enjoying the moment alone it could provide.

When I open the back door, Jeremy is there, a smoke hanging from his mouth and a guilty look on his face.

"Shit, I thought you were Jordyn."

I grin. "So, baby girl moves in and you already have to hide from her to have a smoke in your own place? You out here hiding from a ninety-five-pound girl?"

"Damn right, I am. Don't call her that, you make her sound like a little kid."

"So? We all know she's a grownup, she works here! Besides, compared to some of us, she *is* pretty young..."

I catch a flash of one of the guiltiest looks I've ever seen cross his face. Friend or not, I step right up to him before I even think about it.

"You. Did. Not."

"I haven't done anything!" he bites back a little too quick, which tells me all I need to know about the problem.

He hasn't done anything, I believe him.

But man, does he want to.

Well, can't fault him for that. I know exactly where he's coming from. I step back, taking a breath of the smoke drifting from his cigarette, letting it calm my cravings.

"Well, aren't we a couple of suckers." I shake my head and lean back against the wall.

"You could have Erika," he says on an exhale.

"You could have Jordyn," I counter.

We say nothing for a long time.

"You're right," he finally says. "We're both fucked."

It's not too much later before we're all piling out to the parking lot, ready to head home. I guess we're getting old, or at least settling down some. Not every night lasts until morning.

"Shoot, I forgot to give Jeremy the info I grabbed at work for him." Tav stops just as we get out the door.

"I'll run in with you. I'm gonna hit the bathroom," Matt says. Tav looks at me since it's just Jules and me left in the lot. I'm sure he doesn't want her out here alone.

"No worries. I got your girl while you're gone…" I put my arm around her and Tavish flicks me hard on the knuckles. I just laugh, and they head in.

"I worry about you, Twiz."

"I know, babe. I'm good though."

"You're lying."

I nod. "I'm lying. But I'm not the worst."

She seems to accept that, which for some reason makes me keep talking

"I never did, you know."

"You never what?" Jules looks at me so honestly, it kills me. She could make any man spill all his secrets.

"I never did stop myself from falling in love. I just had to stop her."

She seems to think on that for a moment.

"I think you were too late."

"She'll get over it."

"Why? Why do this to you both? You're a great guy, Twiz, and you made her happy."

"I can't, Jules. I just can't. She deserves someone who can."

Jules opens her mouth but then closes it. Instead, she latches her tiny little body around me in a hug. Which doesn't seem to end and wears me right down until I'm hugging her back with probably more strength than someone that small should receive. I'm just starting to feel a very unwelcome sting in my nose as my eyes fill when I'm saved by a loud growl from a large, mildly annoyed soldier behind me.

And because I'm an asshole like that, I don't let go. Instead, I just look up at him and wink, which only earns me a scowl. He doesn't move any more than that, though, and he seems to be able to tell that I need a minute. He backs off until I feel like I can step back without looking like the loser who almost started crying because a girl told him he deserved something he couldn't have.

When I let go, however, he still pulls her under his arm with a little more possessiveness than warranted, but I'll give it to him.

You don't get that kind of love every day.

"Don't be a caveman, Slick." He just growls at her again and pulls her to the car.

"See you Monday, Twiz. Gimme a call if you're bored this weekend."

I hate that I know that's code for "give me a call if you feel like jumping," but I appreciate the sentiment.

Matt and I jump in my truck and head home. I think we might almost make it there without any uncomfortable conversation, but a few minutes before home, he can't keep quiet.

"The pills, the appointments... it doesn't make you weak, Twiz."

"Ya, it does. I'll just have to live with that."

"No, it doesn't. It makes you human."

"Oh ya? Tavish lost his best friend. Jason lost part of his fucking body. What did I lose, huh?"

Matt waits a moment, and we pull into the driveway, I think

that maybe he doesn't have an answer for that truth, but he finally speaks up.

"You. You lost you."

I just shake my head but as he gets out of the truck, he says, "What's not fair is if we have to lose you, too. You didn't have to go it alone there and you don't have to here, either. Let us in, Twiz."

I head to bed, and I'm out as soon as my head hits the pillow. I feel like I haven't even fallen asleep yet when I am woken by the shrill ring next to my head. I have no idea what time it is, and I glance at my clock as I reach for the phone.

One in the morning.

I don't think there's anything good that ever comes from a phone call at one in the morning. At a glance at the number, the only thing I recognize is the Saskatchewan area code.

When I answer, I barely even say hello. I just wait for whatever bad news is coming.

"Robert Portier?"

My full, birth name has me sit up. I can't even remember the last time I heard it.

"Sampson," it's the automatic response honed from the years after I changed it. "But ya. This is me."

"This is Meggie Fraizer, I'm your Uncle Alan Portier's nurse."

I blink a few times. I haven't seen Alan in years. I can't even remember how long it has been since I went back to my hometown. The only family I had left there was Alan, and neither of us cared for the other's company.

"Okay."

"I'm sorry to tell you this, dear, but it's your uncle. He has taken a turn for the worse. I'm afraid he only has a matter of days. Maybe hours, to be honest."

I stare at the blankets in front of me as I try to process. Alan was long divorced and as far as I had heard, never remarried or had kids.

"I, uh, didn't realize he was sick.

She takes a moment. "I know, and I'm sorry you didn't know sooner. He didn't want me to call. He didn't want to see anyone. But he's not long left for this world, Robert, so I couldn't not call some kind of family..."

I try to picture my uncle, but I always just see my dad. He looked so much like him, always with a cigarette hanging out of his mouth, a scowl on his face, a bottle in his hand.

"Hello, Robert?"

"Sorry, yes, I'll get there as soon as I can. I will probably drive so I should be there by morning. Who should I contact when I arrive?"

"That's me, dear. There's no big rush. Drive safely. I'll give you my number for when you arrive, and I have the keys to the trailer here. He gave them to me so you can..."

Right.

That was the other reason I never thought about visiting.

Uncle Alan was living in the same trailer I grew up in. I'd left it there empty when I enlisted and soon, he'd asked to move in, offering to keep it up for me, and I'd more than agreed. I hadn't wanted to deal with it at the time.

I guess I hadn't put together that I would still have to deal with it someday.

Which, I guess, is today.

"I'll be staying in a hotel," I bark a little harsher than necessary.

"Oh, you don't have to, dear. Alan hasn't been at the trailer in a long time while he has been in the hospital, and the keys are here. His home care nurse told me she had tidied the place up..."

"No!" I take a breath. It's not her fault. "No, thank you, Meggie, was it? It's okay. I appreciate it, but I'd rather just have a hotel room," or sleep in my truck or even in the field out back.

Literally anywhere but there, but I don't add that. "Thank you for calling. What's, uh, what's wrong with him?"

""He has cancer, dear. In his colon, but it spread everywhere before they found it. There was nothing they could do but make him comfortable. Which, for your uncle, mostly just involved a lot of whiskey until he made it to the end."

That sounds about right.

"Okay, I can leave here soon. I'll call when I get into town. If something happens on the way, you can reach me on my cell phone."

I rattle off a number for her and hang up, spending a long time staring at the ceiling before I grab my backpack and shove some clothes in, pulling on a pair of jeans and a hoodie, and hitting the bathroom before walking out to the kitchen.

When I get out there, it's half past one and Matt is sitting at the kitchen table, a cup of coffee in his hand.

"I'd ask why you're up, but I'm too happy that you've made coffee," I say as I fill a giant travel mug.

"Couldn't sleep."

That's bullshit. Who drinks coffee at one in the morning if they're trying to sleep? But I only have time for my own drama at the moment, so I let it go.

"I have to go home," I say, and he looks up surprised.

"For Thanksgiving?" I had completely forgotten it was Thanksgiving weekend. That's better, actually. Gives me some more time.

"Nah, my uncle is dying."

Matt just stares at me open mouthed, and I don't blame him. I never, ever talk about my family.

"I'm sorry?" I don't blame the question in his words, either. The little I do say has never been positive.

"He's old, had cancer awhile apparently. There's no other family so I guess I need to make arrangements. And since the trailer he lives in belongs to me, I guess I have to figure that out, too."

Matt nods and thankfully reads me well enough to let it go at that.

"I'm sure we can get you some time to deal with all that. I'll let you know."

"I guess living with the boss pays off now and again, hey?" I say, trying to keep things light, and he laughs.

"Don't get used to it."

I start to get my boots on, and Matt calls my name from the kitchen. When I look up, he tosses my pills at me from where I had left them on the coffee table.

"Right. Uh, thanks."

"Hey, Twiz?"

I look back as I open the door.

"You're not alone."

I just nod, looking away before he can read the emotion on my face.

I pull into town around breakfast time. The same cheap hotel that's been here since forever in front of my truck, looks the same as every hotel in every town on the prairies. Mostly just there for the bar underneath, it houses some of the coal workers not interested in anything more than a cheap place to lay their heads, and usually that's about it. No one has their family or friends stay in a place like this, but I've slept in worse. When it comes time to deal with the trailer, it will be more convenient than making the daily drive from Estevan. I consider doing what I thought and sleeping in the back of the truck, but it's getting cold out and a hot shower is probably one of the few things this place does provide. I head inside and book for a few nights. I don't know how long it will take to sort things here, but I doubt that, as much as I want to, I'd be able to do it in a day.

Once I'm situated in my room, I pick up the discoloured

phone on the bookcase and dial the number Meggie gave me. I reach the desk of the hospital who patch me to Meggie and as she answers, it occurs to me this woman should not still be working.

"Shouldn't you get off work sometime?" I ask after I've identified myself and letting her know I'm in town. She just laughs.

"I was off awhile back. Was hoping I'd catch you. Alan is still hanging in there, but I'd come down to the hospital as soon as you can. We have him comfortable in our palliative care room. I'll wait."

I hang up with my stomach grumbling, but it looks like I'm headed straight to the hospital. I grab a Snickers from the vending machine on the way out, only flinching a little bit when the chocolate is slightly white on the edges. I have no idea how long it's been in that machine, but I'm sure I've eaten worse. I just shove it in and head out.

Every street, every landmark, every sign reminds me of my childhood, and it already feels heavy just breathing the air. Even the road out of town that takes me to the closest hospital reminds me of every summer night as a teenager, desperate to leave to what we called the city back then, though now seems so small and not the exciting hotspot it appeared to a bunch of small-town kids.

I get to the hospital and once I park, I take a moment to grab a few deep breaths and remember the pills Matt threw to me when I see them sitting on my passenger seat. It's like a sign, since I should be taking one about now. I swallow it back with the cold coffee I picked up at a Tim's before I crossed out of Alberta and walk in the door.

The nurses don't have to ask me when I get to the counter, who I'm looking for. I knew they wouldn't. I look just like him because he looks just like my dad. Even if there was some question, since I'm much younger and who knows how my uncle looks now, I just have to look at them.

My whole life, doctors have argued about whether hete-rochromia was inherited from your parents or not, but no matter what they said, it couldn't change the fact that soon after I was born, only one of my blue eyes turned brown. Just like my father's.

Since then, I got to hear how cool it was and how interesting we both had different-coloured eyes, and how it made us so much alike.

Later, though, once he was finally gone, it became a reminder to everyone that I was his son, and *just like him*.

That's not the kind of thing you outrun in a small town. Which is made clear by these older women at the counter when they flinch when they see me, and hurry to page Meggie.

No matter how often people tell me how cool my eyes are, they'll always just be his.

I don't even remember what colour eyes my Uncle Alan has, but they weren't the same as his brother's. That doesn't change the fact that even all these years later, the nurses look at me and know right away. They know who Alan is, who his brother was, and so they know who I am.

They don't need to finish paging her. Meggie comes out of the office when she hears the nurse greet me. A short, curvy woman in probably her late fifties, with a giant smile and even bigger blond hair, she rushes right over to me.

"You must be Robert." I open my mouth to correct her, but I don't. Robert works here. For some reason, I don't want this town to call me Twiz.

"Come, Alan is down this way."

We walk down the hall, and I hear the whispers start before we even turn the corner. Meggie turns around and gives a look that makes *me* want to apologize, before turning back to me.

"Don't you mind those busy bodies. If they have nothing better to talk about after this long, that says more about them than anything else, doesn't it?"

I say nothing. I've only been in this town an hour and some-how, I am a seventeen-year-old kid again, *his* son that no one is safe around.

Meggie didn't get that memo, apparently. She puts her arm around me as we turn to Alan's door and the gentle gesture catches me off guard. She doesn't skip a beat, though.

"He's in and out, dear. He might be able to talk, he might not. I'm surprised he's stuck around with us this long. I'll be right out there if you need me."

"You've done enough. You should go home…" She smiles.

"This is why I do this job, my dear. My Harvey will be fine heating up spaghetti from the fridge for his lunch. I'll stay a little longer."

I'm so grateful to have someone here on my side, I don't even argue. I just walk into the door, completely unsure what to expect. If anything, I thought there would be a half-dozen machines, beeping and monitors flashing, but it's just a very small, very frail-looking man in a room with nothing more than a small IV line. There's a couch against one wall and a TV; it's a special room put together for families to spend the last days with their loved ones.

I don't know if I'd call Alan a loved one, but I might be the closest he's got.

I sit on the chair by his bed and take a good look at the man I have avoided looking at since I was a teenager.

His hair is long and stringy, patchy and thin on his head. His cheeks are sunken, and his eyes seem to be too far back in his head. Under the blanket, his frame is so much smaller than I've ever remembered. I know some of that must be the cancer, but part of it is probably also the twisted memories of how a child sees a monster.

Younger only by ten months, Alan could have passed as my father's twin when he was alive and that alone was enough to earn my fear as a child. The fact that him and my dad were always together, inseparable, and that he would watch and encourage my dad for 'teaching me a lesson' anytime he got the chance, that only made it worse

As I settle in my chair, Alan opens his eyes and the first thing I notice is the yellow.

The second, that they're brown.

"Robbie."

I flinch at the name my father used. I'd even rather Robert, but I don't bother correcting him. It doesn't seem worth his last moments. His scratchy voice sounds like the pain it probably causes him to speak, and he motions to a cup of water with a straw near his bed that I pass him. After taking a tiny sip, he has me put it back.

"I didn't tell them to call you."

"Well, they did."

We say nothing else for a long while.

"You'll be the last Portier left."

"I haven't been a Portier in a long time."

He scoffs at me, which causes him to cough for a few minutes.

"I heard you changed it. Surprised me you picked that *girl's* name and not hers. "

"That *girl* was the woman who birthed me. I didn't deserve to take Mom's name."

His old weathered face tried to scowl but can't quite get there.

"Name or not, I'll be gone, and you'll be the last one."

"That name will die with you, Alan, and no one will mourn it." It's a harsh answer, but I didn't come here to pretend we were ever family.

"You're probably right."

He says nothing for a while, his eyes close again and I wonder if he's fallen back asleep. I'd wonder if he was just dead, but I can still hear his shallow breathing.

"You look just like my brother. God, I miss him."

"I'm nothing like him."

"Be that as it may, you look just like he did when he died. You've always looked like him. He was a good brother."

"He was a monster."

He scoffs again, this time it's almost like his body is too tired to cough.

"We are who we are. If he was a monster, what does that make us? What does it make me? What does it make you, Robbie?"

With that, he does fall back asleep. I wonder if he'll wake up again, if he hung on just to say that to me and what kind of person does that? I hear a soft voice behind me.

"You are not your father, Robert. Or Alan. Appearance doesn't make it so. You are who you chose to be."

She sits on the chair next to me, and we listen to his ragged and sporadic breathing.

When she pats my knee what feels like hours later, I realize I'm crying.

By mid-afternoon, they unhook his IV and cover his face.

I sign a couple of papers, and Meggie gives me his belongings, a battered key on a ring, the only one that matters.

I know what I need to do.

I've made the phone call before I even leave the funeral home parking lot.

22

ERIKA

I have fed nine people a turkey dinner I made, and I don't think I poisoned anyone.

I could not possibly be more impressed with myself.

It's only just after lunchtime on Saturday but after our afternoon meal, the group of us are hardly even talking; digesting takes so much effort. There's still half of a pie on the table, along with ten bottles of wine and other liquor since I told them all not to bring food. Less than half are empty, though, and I think we are too full even to drink.

My dad is on the biggest leather chair by the TV, flipping through American football games, while Tav, Jason, and Beth are on the couch. Jules sits on pillows on the floor, insisting it's more comfortable, much to her husband's annoyance that she wouldn't take his spot on the couch. Jeremy and Jordyn are on dining chairs that we pulled into the circle. I'm puttering in the kitchen. Matt wanders to the hall to take a phone call.

"Ugh. Erika, seriously. I can't breathe." Juliette flops from her spot cross legged to a starfish on the floor, and Tavish playfully taps her comically protruding, food-stuffed belly with his foot.

"You look pregnant," he jokes, and Juliette freezes, her eyes wide.

Tavish furrows his brow and glances at her glass of plain cranberry juice on the table.

"Shit." Juliette scrambles up. "Shit! I wanted to tell you tonight. I mean… Shit!" At that, everyone else in the room whoops and laughs, and Tavish is still sitting there on the couch like a deer in headlights.

Slowly, he gets up but drops to his knees on the floor in front of Jules, looking up at her.

"Are you pregnant?" he whispers. She just nods furiously, her eyes red. He wraps his arms around her from his position below, his head resting on her belly, and the room goes silent. Then, all at once, he's up, lifting her off the ground and hollering, "I'm having a baby!"

There's much backslapping and happy tears from the girls and smiles all around, but as Jason heads to the kitchen to pour a celebratory round of drinks for everyone but Juliette, Matt comes back from where he was in the hall and stops him.

"I know it's bad timing…" Everyone looks over. There's a fear on their faces I don't place until I remember that in their world, they have brothers still at war.

"Twiz called. He needs us."

Jason just nods, putting the bottle down.

"He's home in Saskatchewan. I'm going to leave now. I can be there before midnight."

Jason grabs his jacket.

"I'll join you."

"I'm going to do my best to be back here before work on Tuesday…" Matt says, and I'm too busy processing how they can already be moving this fast.

Why is Twiz in Saskatchewan? What's wrong? Most importantly, can I go too?

"We'll figure all that out on the way. Let me head home and

pack a bag. Meet me at my place when you're ready to go." With that, and a kiss on my cheek, he's out the door, with Beth thanking me for dinner as she follows.

Tavish looks at Juliette, clearly unsure.

"Slick, I'll still be pregnant on Tuesday," she says gently, and he nods, still uncertain, a hand resting protectively on her belly.

"I want Twiz to be here to see our baby." That seems to get him moving.

"Okay, Matt, I'm in too. Let me go home and pack. I'll meet you at your place in a half hour. I'll just leave my truck there." Tav thanks me for dinner and Jules gives me a hug, and they head out after Jason.

"Erika, Jeremy and I can stay and help you clean up. We both have to work tomorrow." I look over at Jordyn who is putting glasses in the sink, but at the same time, Matt shakes his head.

"Erika, come with us."

I get that the Army has taught them all to move fast, but I'm too busy processing. Five minutes ago, I was washing dishes and going to bed before ten.

"If you want to go, sweetie, you should go. This friend of yours seems important, and I like the way he looks at you. I'll stay with these two, and I can lock up when we're done." My dad looks at me kindly, and I don't think I ever thought I'd hear him tell me it was okay to leave him and do something for myself.

I find myself nodding and running to my room, throwing things into a bag and meeting Matt at the front door. Just like that, we're out, and I have hours on the road to think about whether he'll be happy to see me.

I doze softly in the passenger seat that I insisted I didn't need since both Jason and Tavish are bigger than I am, but they wouldn't hear it. None of them say much, other than Matt's rundown of Twiz's call.

His uncle died, that's why he had gone. Apparently, he held

on until after Twiz arrived but not long. Matt doesn't know much about Twiz's family, other than his parents died when he was in his late teens, and he doesn't ever go home.

When he called, all he told Matt was that he wasn't okay. He asked if anyone wanted to take a road trip, and Matt told him he'd be there before the end of the night.

My heart aches at that kind of friendship, the kind that just knows, the kind that drives over eight hours across the prairies because of one single phone call.

It's nearing midnight when we pull into this sleepy town in southern Saskatchewan. I perk up as we drive through it, trying to picture Twiz at the outdoor hockey rink, or even at the bike racks in front of the school. Everything here looks like it's been here for a hundred years, peeling siding and faded paint, even the stoplights look like they came from a different era.

It's something I guess I take for granted in the city, the constant change of businesses, new paint, new signs, growth, change. This town didn't get that memo. There's not much around it, and we're almost two hours from anything resembling a big city, at least by my standards. Even the closest Tim Horton's is in Estevan, and that's almost a half hour from here.

I can't even begin to imagine what it would be like to live here, this little village where it seems like time hasn't touched it in thirty years or more.

Matt slows down, winding around to the address Twiz gave him. It seems like we're lost, or that we're just heading right out of the town when he finally pulls onto a dirt road and in the distance, I see a driveway with Twiz's big-ass truck parked in it.

At least, I'm assuming it's a driveway. It's mostly just a slightly mowed-down spot in a lot filled with rocks and some dead weeds. It's eerily dark, darker than I think it's even capable of being anywhere near the city, with only the faint glow of the highway streetlights behind us and the headlights of Matt's car and Twiz's truck illuminating a rundown trailer.

There's a figure sitting on the hood of Twiz's truck. He doesn't even turn to the sound of the crunch of the car on the gravel. Considering how dark and still the night is, he probably could have heard us coming for miles. He gives no indication that he does, though. He's just sitting on the hood, staring.

Matt takes a deep breath as he shuts off the engine, and without the sound of the motor, the silence is deafening. None of us move at first, and Jason is the first to click his seatbelt off and open the door, the rest of the guys close behind. I get out slowly, staying behind them as they approach him as though he's a bomb set to go off anytime.

The lights of Matt's car haven't turned off yet, and they illuminate Twiz and the bottle of Black Velvet in his one hand, his other holding... a lighter? He's not smoking though. I don't think I've ever seen him have a cigarette.

"Welcome to my home." He breaks the silence, finally looking over at us and I see the complete desperation on his face just a moment before the car's headlights automatically shut off and, with the only other light coming from Twiz's truck in front of him, he's bathed in thick darkness.

He takes a swig from the bottle and passes it over to the boys, who each take a small sip. I almost pass, but this seems like a ritual I can't skip. Twiz's eyes widen just a moment when he sees me step forward to reach for the bottle.

"Hellcat." His strangled voice holds a tone I can't decipher and I'm not sure if he's happy to see me, or angry. Or if he even knows.

"Twiz." Jason is the first of us to speak, as he passes the bottle back to Twiz.

"No one here calls me that. Isn't that weird? They call me Robert. Alan, he called me Robbie, but I guess now that he's gone, no one calls me that anymore."

Robbie sounds like a little boy's name, and I would never think to attach it to the man I know Twiz to be. It's hard for me to think of him as anything but the strong, almost invincible soldier I know he is. The one who would stand against a doorway to protect me from whatever comes through.

I have heard his stories, on our runs when he would tell me about his deployments and his experiences. Never in those times did he seem small, or weak, or broken. Even through his panic some days, he never seemed anything but strong to me.

Right now, though, he looks defeated.

"My mom wasn't really my mom. I mean, she was, but she didn't give birth to me." As he starts talking, we all just adjust our little circle, so we can listen.

"The woman who did was a sixteen-year-old named Georgina Sampson. My dad was twenty-one, already living in this trailer and working at the coal mine, when he knocked her up. From what people told me when I was older, he loved her desperately. She hid her pregnancy a long time, I guess, scared her parents would disown her and he'd leave her. She was right about her parents. They threw her out when she was so far along she couldn't hide it anymore. My dad, though, from what I hear, he was happy. He moved her in with him, said he'd marry her once I was born, but he never got the chance. She died about an hour after I made my appearance. I guess she started hemorrhaging, and they couldn't stop it. Dad told me her parents showed up at the hospital and when they heard she was gone, they walked out without a word, moved back to Regina, and never even asked to see me."

There's already tears down my face, but Twiz is emotionless, staring at the old trailer in front of him. Tavish grabs the bottle from the bumper and takes another, deeper drink from it, his face souring at the taste. The only sounds are the trucks on the highway in the distance.

"Alan told me once that Dad lost it at the hospital. He had to be sedated when they told him Georgina was dead. The crazy part is he kept me, brought me back to the trailer to the room they already had set up. I never got why, except I was a part of her he couldn't let go of. I don't remember much about those first years. I have no idea how he managed to keep me alive when it sounds like all he did was drink and work. He was an asshole, quick with his temper and his belt. I'll never know if it was who he was before or if it was losing Georgina that did it. All I know is he hated me and made sure I knew it, until one day around my tenth birthday, he married Louise and she adopted me.

"That should be a happy story, right? Louise was amazing, having her saved my life. I was sure of it. For a little while, Dad was happy and didn't hurt me. We were a family, and having a mom was everything.

"She had long, blond hair that she'd brush out at night while she read me stories before bed. She was quiet, you know, soft spoken, never lost her temper. She taught kindergarten at the school here. That's why she moved from Saskatoon. Eventually, she and Dad had my two brothers. Sam was born when I was twelve, and Steven was born when I was sixteen. Three boys plus Dad in the house, and she was still just so gentle. She was like a fairytale mom.

"Right up until Dad killed her."

23

TWIZ

$\mathcal{I}$ never should have let Dad marry her.

Oh, he was good for a while. He doted on her when they were dating. They seemed genuinely good together. Then, she got pregnant with Sam and something about that made him snap. I would lie in bed listening to them fight, terrified she'd leave me alone with him again. She didn't leave, though, no matter how often Dad screamed at her for nothing at all. He had this game where he would refuse to tell her what he wanted for dinner and then smack her around when she'd serve him the wrong thing. The worst was at night when I'd hear her sob through the thin walls of the room I shared with Sam while he'd be doing God knows what to her. Usually Sam would crawl in bed with me and I'd hold him against my chest with my hand over his ears so he couldn't hear, and he'd fall asleep.

I should have done something to stop it and get her out, but I was selfish. I wanted a mom. So, I'd just try to take the brunt of his punishments, which wasn't hard. He hated me, and he liked to let me know. He hated that I didn't look like my birth mom.

He said that when he kept me, he wanted her son to look like her, but all I ever managed to look like was him.

He hated me for killing Georgina simply by being born, and he hated that I ever had any of Louise's attention. He didn't want me stealing another woman from him.

As I got older and tried to protect Louise and Sam, I would antagonize him. Poke at everything I knew would get his attention just so I'd be the one who felt his belt and not them. I want to say it was because I wanted to protect her, but I think deep down, it was also because I was scared she would leave him and wouldn't take me with her.

Then I got bigger, so I thought maybe I could stay with Louise and we could just get rid of him together. The last time he hit me was around when I turned sixteen. I came home from a date with some girl and he accused me of sleeping with her, ranting how he wouldn't have any bastard baby of mine in his house. He threw the first punch and without thinking, I knocked him on his ass. He didn't say a word, just got up and walked away from me. After that, he never raised his hand to me again, and not to the others in front of me, either. I know she was still scared, though, and at night, I know he hurt her where I couldn't see. I desperately wanted to save her like she saved me.

During my last year in high school, things got worse. When the baby was born, Dad seemed to melt down even more. It seemed like he was never sober, and he was eventually fired from his job for showing up one too many times too drunk to work. The trailer was owned free and clear, which is the only reason we never ended up kicked out on our ass, since Louise by then was on maternity leave with the Steven.

I tried so many times to convince her to walk away then. I knew I couldn't stay once school was done. I planned to be out the door as soon as I was eighteen, and I wanted her to leave with me. I couldn't protect her if I left, but I so badly knew I couldn't stay. She'd keep saying it wasn't like I thought, that he never hurt her too badly, that once the baby was born, once she could work and they weren't broke, once he found a new job... She was always waiting for whatever it was she thought would make it better. She stopped saying that she was staying because she loved him, though. I took that as a sign, and I started looking for places we could move to together once I got a job. She'd never listen, always tell me to just plan for *my* future, that she'd be okay, that she'd protect the boys, that Dad would get better soon, as though he was sick or something. She would never agree to come with me, and I'd never agree to go without her.

I should have known he had finally gone too far that week. He was following Louise around when she'd go into town. The night before, he had been mumbling to himself how she thought she could leave him. I dismissed it as more of his drunken ramblings, but maybe she was. Maybe she was planning to leave without me; maybe she didn't want me there. I wasn't really hers, you know? I will never know what she said to him, if it was anything at all. All I know is that for some reason, he snapped that day.

THE POLICE OFFICER won't let go, and it takes another to hold on, to stop me from making it to her. They don't get me out of the room in time, though, before I see someone in a uniform gently lift Mom's prone figure and take something from underneath. A small, dripping red bundle.

Steven.

He looks like a doll from a horror movie, his entire body covered in blood. I don't know if it's his or hers, but it doesn't matter. He's not moving, not making a sound. The man holding him is in no hurry; that can only mean there's nothing to hurry for.

"Robert, please, come out here with us. Is there someone we can call?"

There's no one to call. My whole family is in that trailer and none of them are moving.

"Where is he?" I croak at the officer.

"Who, son?"

"My father. Where is he?"

"We haven't seen your dad, Robert. Do you have reason to believe he would be here?"

I just stare at them incredulously. "Of course I do. Who do you think did this?"

The officers look at each other. "Well, we don't know that yet, Robert. We just arrived on the scene a little while ago, following a report of gunshots from the neighbours. We haven't seen anyone else."

"He's here somewhere." My voice is dead. There's no rush to find him, it won't bring them back. My whole family was in that trailer. My whole life...

"Sergeant! We have another body."

I look up to the sound of an officer running from the back.

"Male, middle-aged, found him in the back in a truck. Looks like a gunshot wound to the head, the gun is still in the vehicle."

With that knowledge that he's gone, my body collapses. The police think that it's because I'm devastated at my father's death, that maybe we were close, that maybe we planned this together.

The truth is I'm just both angry and grateful I won't have to kill the bastard myself.

When I finish telling the story, no one says a word for a long time, and I don't know if it's because they're disgusted or angry or hurt. I decide to just go on.

"Social services got involved eventually. Uncle Alan didn't want me, couldn't look after me, not with the amount of drinking he was doing. I didn't have anyone else. Definitely not Louise's family. They lived in the city and the only time I saw them after it happened was as I stood on the edge of the funeral they held for her and my brothers. Her dad walked right over to me and told me I was not welcome, called me the 'bastard son of a murderer' and accused me of letting her die. The cop that was nearby, he was the one that had helped me when it happened. He told me to give them time, but they never contacted me again, and they told Child Services that I wasn't their grandchild, and they had no interest in a 'further relationship' as the social worker put it.

"They placed me with a local family who were nice enough, if not a little standoffish around me, so I could finish school, but I never did. I don't know how they thought I could. The news ran with the story. National, international. The small-town monster with the beautiful life that mowed down his whole family before he took the coward's way out. They'd always linger on me in the story, the "half-brother" that was spared. They all had theories why, maybe I was the favourite? Maybe I was in on it? Truth was I have no idea why he did it, or why he didn't wait until I was home, why he left me behind, but I think I have a good idea. When he would whip me with his belt in my room, he always complain that he was wasting his energy, that he should just kill me and get it over with, but then he'd always say the same thing.

"I wasn't worth the bullet to him."

At this, I hear Erika audibly flinch, like the sound of her body retreating can actually be heard in the night. I rush the rest of the story out before they're gone.

"Everyone hated me. Or was scared of me. I'd been asked to leave stores, told 'they didn't want any trouble.' People would avoid me on the street, the few friends I had wouldn't even make eye contact with me in the halls. I was, from that moment on, *his son*. And by association, capable of the same violence.

"The trailer and land were mine, but not until I turned eighteen, and I never wanted to see it again anyways. I had a shitty old car I had bought when I got my license the year before, and I used it to drive back and forth to the recruiting center in Regina, take the tests, all that shit. The day I turned eighteen, I signed it all myself and waited. They called me with a job offer for the infantry less than a week later. I was the only person alone at my swearing in. I never went back home, just slept in the car in Regina until the day I left, when I sold it for a dollar to some teenager and got on the bus. I changed my name within the year to my birth mom's. I could never be a Langlois. I didn't deserve my mom's name. It felt fitting that the teenager that died bringing me into the world would give me her name when I was left alone again.

"I let Alan live in the trailer in exchange for keeping it up for me. I didn't care. I never planned on ever coming back here. I thought if I ran far enough, I could get away forever. Maybe if I served my country, I could atone for what he did. It took some convincing, but when I was twenty-one, I even got a doctor to give me a vasectomy. That way I knew I couldn't ever endanger a child's life like my father had. I knew it meant I'd be alone, but I always thought it meant maybe I'd keep far enough away from here, from relationships, from any kind of chance I'd become the legacy everyone thought I would.

"Yet, here I am."

The silence is a heavy weight around me when I'm done talking. Jason leans against the hood of the car and gives a deep exhale. Tav clenches his fists at his side and cracks his knuckles. Erika just stands and stares. I'm sure now that she knows, she wishes she was back at her safe home where she can forget she ever let a man like me in her bed.

"Twiz, all of that, all of it, is all kinds of fucked up. You didn't deserve that. No one does. You are nothing, nothing like that. You have to know that." Matt's voice has the tone he uses when he's talking to his troops when they're in trouble.

"And yet, a few months ago, I killed a young woman in cold blood."

Matt blinks. But his eyes don't turn to pity, or disgust, like I thought they would. Instead, they blaze with anger.

"You. Saved. My. Life."

"I could have found another way."

"No." This time it's Tavish's voice, an ice-hard tone I haven't heard before. "No, you couldn't have. I was your partner, and the call was as much mine as yours. It sucked, and I'm sorry you're the one who had to pull the trigger, but there was no other way."

I hang my head. I don't have an answer to that. I just know I can't be trusted.

Erika steps forward, and I brace myself for her to lash out, hit me, express her disgust that I let myself get so close to her knowing what I was capable of.

Instead, she steps right between my open legs where I'm sitting on the hood of my truck and wraps her arms around me, resting her head on my shoulder a moment. I can't move my own arms. They're like weights at my side, but she keeps holding on. When she lets go, she backs up only a little bit and cups her hands on my face, running her thumbs over the scruff of the weekend's growth on my chin.

She shakes her head. "I love you." I open my mouth to object, but she just presses it closed.

"I loved you when I'd watch you teach women how to protect themselves. I loved you when I ran beside you in the river valley. I loved you when I'd be drunk with you at the pub. I loved you when I was hiding in my closet at my condo as you stood at the doorway, ready to take on anyone to protect me." She leans in closer to my ear.

"I loved you when I was lying on my back on my kitchen table in the dark." I hear a snicker behind me that tells me she wasn't as quiet as she intended, but it doesn't matter. She steps back again to face me, her eyes staring in mine.

"I loved you when you protected me from a plastic bag on

the trail. I loved you when you confided in me while we ran. I loved you when you whimpered in your sleep and I would press my head against your chest until you quieted."

"I know who you are, Robert Twiz Portier Sampson. You are not him, and I'm not her, and I love you." I feel the tears in my eyes, but I blink them back.

"Didn't you hear me? I can't have kids, Erika."

"Didn't you hear me? I love you. What makes you think I even wanted kids? There are no guarantees for anyone when it comes to that stuff, who says I can even have them? I've never checked, and I've never cared to. I have no interest in children of my own. I never have. If I do one day, if we both do, there's other ways to go about it anyways. To be honest, right now, a life with just the two of us sounds amazing. You're not hearing me. I. Love. You."

I can't... I can't do this now. I have one more thing to do, one more goodbye. I don't break eye contact with Erika but raise my voice so the guys can hear.

"Thanks for coming. I'm gonna need you in about an hour, but you guys need... you need to head to the hotel. Make sure someone sees you all when you check in."

Matt chuckles behind me, and Tavish digs something from his pocket.

It's a silver lighter, a fancy metal one with something on the front I can't quite see in the dark when he flicks it open and it lights up.

Erika closes her eyes for half a moment before she steps back. Jason puts his arms around me from his spot next to me on the bumper.

"Have you been inside yet?" Matt asks.

I shake my head. "Only to throw a few things in." That gets the same round of chuckles. Tavish grabs the bottle of whiskey off the ground by the tire and takes a long pull, passing it to the rest. Only Matt turns it down.

"You want to go in?" Matt finally asks.

"I want you guys to go. I have something I have to do."

"We figured." Matt opens his trunk and pulls out an emergency kit because of course, he has one. He passes Jason a pack of lighters, still in a plastic case.

"I don't know what you guys think you're doing..."

"Seems to me," Matt says, taking the now opened pack of lighters and keeping one before tossing the rest back in the trunk with the package. Tavish keeps flicking open and closed the damn Bic in his hand.

"You keep saying you have something you need to do."

"Alone. I have something to do alone."

"Twiz, I stood right next to you and told you to take the shot in Kandahar. I'm standing right next to you now, too. You aren't doing shit alone." Tavish's voice is firm.

"I don't know what kind of trouble..."

"What kind of trouble we're all going to be in? We'll deal with it together when it comes."

Tav takes another swig of the whiskey but doesn't back down.

"I'm asking again, you want to look inside one more time?" I stare Matt down but he's not having it. Neither of us is willing to back down, and I take a deep breath.

"No. I don't ever want back in there. I threw in some of the brush that I cleared from around the outside. I didn't go in their room, though. I didn't really look..." He nods and jogs over to the trailer, tugging open the stuck screen door and disappearing inside for a moment. He's not gone long before he's back.

"It's clear."

"It's never going to be clear. They're all still stuck in there, and I need to let them go."

Tavish steps into the circle, the glow from the lighter illuminating his face.

"Let's light shit up!"

He has the same look on his face he gets before battle over-seas, and when I look at Matt, he does too. I've never seen Jason overseas, but I'd bet that scary as hell look on his face usually only comes out then, too.

Grabbing some brush from the back of the truck, we all light one, like a torch. Erika comes and takes one. I try to stop her but she's having none of it. She lights hers off mine. We walk towards the trailer in silence. Matt heads in a moment, and I see the light of the curtains burn first. As soon as he's out, the rest of us toss our makeshift torches inside. Matt stands next to me and puts his hand on my shoulder.

Standing a distance away and watching, it's barely a flicker inside, and that's when Jason comes out from behind the truck, with the whiskey bottle in his hand and smell of gasoline in the air. Taking off his jacket, he pulls his t-shirt over his head and then calmly zips his jacket back up. He rips a strip off his black shirt and shoves it in the top of the bottle. I realize what he's doing.

"Oh, shit," Tavish says, but he's laughing. We're all laughing, and for a minute, with the faint sounds of the fire in the back-ground, it all seems absurd.

"Fuckers are taking too long. Like no one's ever taught every one of us how to make a damn bomb. You want to do the honours?" He tips the bottle in my direction and I grab it.

We walk as close as is safe, and he picks up a good-size rock from the ground before tossing it at the kitchen window, shat-tering it. Then with a look back to the rest of them, I catch Erika's eyes for a moment before I light the cloth on the bottle and throw it in as hard as I can. Jason and I jog back to the rest of them, the sound of the small explosion behind us, and with the brush I'd dumped in there earlier, it doesn't take long after that. We drive Matt's car and my truck to the very far end of the drive, all five of us finding a spot on top of one as we watch it burn in silence. When Erika rests her head on my shoulder, I realize I'm shaking and for once, I don't try to hide the tears. No one says a word.

It's sooner than I thought it would be when we hear the sirens. This far out, our volunteer department doesn't get out as fast as they would in the city. It doesn't surprise me that the first vehicle up the dirt road is an RCMP car. The closest station is a good half hour away, but they drive through town regularly.

I guess I shouldn't be surprised, either when the cop who gets out of the car is familiar. I can't imagine working over a decade in the same small-town detachment, but this officer looks close to retirement. He's the same one who sat with me through all that needed to be questioned and sorted back then, just a little greyer and significantly rounder.

He shuts his sirens and lights off before he even turns onto the road, and when he parks next to us, he gets out calmly, moving to stand between our two vehicles. I hold Erika a little closer to me as he approaches, and wipe at my face a few times.

"Gentlemen. Ma'am. Mr. Portier."

I had almost hoped he wouldn't remember, but it was the biggest things to happen to this town... ever.

"Sampson. I'm not a Portier."

He regards me a moment before nodding, then looks back to the fire.

"I heard Alan passed today. I'm sorry for your loss, son."

"I'm not."

He gives me the same nod, and it's quiet for a while. Eventually, we hear the faint sounds of the local volunteer fire department trucks in the distance.

"I don't suppose you'd be claiming insurance for this."

"No, sir. I reckon I'll just sell it for the land. I hear some developers are interested."

"Ya, I bet they are. Shame you couldn't have kept the trailer. Then again, I always said that thing was just a fire trap waiting to happen. All that old wood, the gas lines were a bit touchy.

Anyone tried to cook something was probably risking their life. I'm sure Alan mentioned in passing once that he was meaning to have that looked at."

I don't have anything to say to that, so I say nothing. When the fire truck pulls up, he walks over to them, and they're slow to move, eventually spraying down first the ground around the trailer before extinguishing the fire in the trailer itself. I can't tell how long we sit and watch. The sun is just starting to peek a red haze in the distance when they sift through the charred remains for hot spots and finally, the RCMP officer walks back over.

"Sergeant." I nod at him.

"I'm the detachment commander now, actually."

"Congratulations." He shrugs.

"It's not the chief of the Toronto PD or anything, but it's not without its perks. You all have somewhere to stay?"

"Yes, sir. I have a room in town. Might head with my friends to Estevan for the night, though. That room isn't the most comfortable for two."

He laughs. "No one takes a girl they want to keep to the town hotel, son." He pulls out his pad and I sit up straight, waiting for whatever trouble is coming. I know none of them are experts, but I'm guessing a trailer full of burned brush and smashed glass are some pretty harsh clues.

"I don't see any reason for an investigation without an insurance claim, especially since we can all just be grateful the place didn't go up with Alan in it. Good timing, I figure, eh, boys? I will have to take some information on the witnesses, just so you can let me know what you did when you came on the trailer and it was burning."

Everyone else gives their names, IDs, and contact info. Tavish and Jason head to Matt's car so they can see about getting us all a place to crash in Estevan for what's left of the early morning, and the officer sits on the hood next to me while

Matt grabs Erika a ranger blanket from the back of my truck as she sits in the passenger seat.

"This is a lot more paperwork than I like, son."

"Sorry, sir."

He sighs, a long deep exhale, and drops his head. "I figure it's about time this town let it go. It probably did me a favour, burning like this. Worse thing I've seen in my career, not just what we found inside that place, but the teenager we didn't know how to help. Still weighs me down, you know, picturing those kids, wondering what became of their brother."

My eyes go up when he calls me 'their brother' instead of 'his son.'

"Maybe without this old trailer haunting us, we can *all* move on." He slaps my shoulder and gets up.

"Go get some rest, son. I'll be in touch if I need you, but I don't anticipate I will."

I stand, my legs stiff under me, the alcohol all burned out of my system in the hours we've been sitting here. The fire trucks are just pulling out the drive and Sergeant Markenson gives me a nod before he drives away.

I take a last look at the remains of the trailer I grew up in and Matt comes around the front to me, putting his hand out to pull me to my feet. We walk to the doors.

With one last glance, I let myself believe what I've wanted my whole life.

This isn't my home.

24

ERIKA

"*I* can't believe I didn't know this about you!" I try for the tenth time to change the dial on the radio, but he just smacks my hand away again.

"It's the only kind of music to listen to! My truck, my station!" I pull out my most exaggerated sigh.

"I can't take any more twang, Twiz. You don't even listen to the good kind of country music!"

"You just think that's the good kind because it sounds like pop music!"

"I can't take one more Corb Lund song!"

We've been having the same argument for three hundred kilometers, and there's still four hundred more to go. If he doesn't change the station, I don't think I'll make it.

Tavish, Jason, and Matt headed back home on Monday morning, after spending most of Sunday sleeping and lazing around the little city, grabbing food and watching movies in the boys' room.

I called my Dad and took the week off, staying with Twiz while he finished the final arrangements for his uncle and listed the lot the trailer was on for sale. He had an offer by the next day, and everything was all but sold by the time we pulled out of town this morning. Turns out, there was more than one developer hoping to get their hands on that piece, since even though the trailer was small, it sat on an entire section of land. It was the only inheritance Twiz had, and he'd never considered that on its sale, it meant he would be sitting on a good chunk of money.

"Are you going to buy a house?"

"Maybe, eventually. I'm going to need a new job soon, though."

"From what Matt tells me, you have lots of time, Twiz. They're not going to throw you out next month."

"No, they're not. I could keep fighting. Honestly, Hellcat, I just think I'm done. My counsellor on base, she's assured me that I have a ways to go, and I'll manage the issues. I can try different medications if this one doesn't work, and there's groups I can go to and all that. I'll probably end up with some cash for it regardless, and I could wait to see if I can stay in, or if they'll medically release me but... I think leaving the Army will be my choice."

I sit on that for a moment. It's hard to picture Twiz as anything but a soldier, but he seems like he's spent a lot of time thinking this through.

"I'm not going to decide today, but I've been thinking on it a long time, even before this money showed up. I think I'd like to start a gym. A fitness gym but one that also offers classes on self-defence for women. Personal trainers, that kind of thing."

"Probably not tomorrow, but one day."

I don't add to that. I'm proud of him for seeing a future out of the military when I know leaving was never his plan.

"What would you call it? Twiz's Training?"

"Um, no." He chuckles.

"You know what's funny?" I muse. "I've never asked you what Twiz means."

At this, he laughs, a full body laugh that makes his eyes water.

"It's not as good of a story as you probably think it is."

"Well, I'm sure it's something heroic, since you got it in the military, right?"

He laughs harder. I think he might have to pull over.

"It's been so long now it's just a name to me. I never think about where it came from.

"So, on my first deployment, we got bored at camp, making stupid bets, you know. Most of them getting people to eat something crazy. Well, someone had sent a care package to one of the other guys, and it was full of those long, red licorice candies, you know? Probably a good ten to fifteen packages. One of the guys, he knows I love them, and he bets a bunch of cash that I can't eat it all. Then they were all pitching money in to get me to do it."

"You're not serious?"

"Yup. So, I do, because of course I do. I get it down fast so that my body doesn't have time to think. I take the cash on the table and make it mayyyybe ten feet and bleh." He makes an exaggerated puking noise. "All over, this bright-red puke, every-where. There was so much of it too, there was no way to stop it. So gross." He laughs at the memory, even as I'm turning green at the thought.

"Took me and the guys forever to hose everything down, clean all the bedding and shit. After that, those guys called me Twiz. After a while, it was all anyone called me. Most of the guys now, they probably don't even know why. To this day, still can't eat them. Which sucks, because they are delicious."

I just shake my head. "You're right. I'm going back to pretending it was something heroic."

He glances my way and smiles. "Sure, babe, whatever makes me look best."

The song on the radio changes and I try desperately one last time to make it stop, but he's quick to cover the dial with his free hand.

"I can't believe you like this. You're terrible."

"You love me," he says, and I know it came out without thinking, but as soon as it's out there, he can't take it back, and we both freeze.

"I do," I say, since when else should we have an awkward conversation about our feelings than in an eight-hour car ride alone together.

He's quiet for a long time, too long, and I start to do some math on how long exactly we would have to go without talking for it to be okay to talk about something entirely different when someone finally says something.

"I love you too."

His voice is calm, but he's staring at the road, like he doesn't even know I'm in the truck.

"I'm sorry, did you just tell me you love me for the first time while looking at roadkill?"

"I'm driving, Erika. What do you want me to do?"

"You can't just tell someone you love them for the first time without even looking at them when you say it!"

"FINE!" Twiz pulls the truck over and turns on the hazards, gets out, and I see him storm around the front, opening my door while blocking the completely empty highway from me with his body. He undoes my seatbelt, hauls me out and all but drags me to the other side of the vehicle before pushing my back against it and caging me in on both sides with his arms. He's breathing heavy by the time we stop there in that position, and I look up into his eyes, the heat in them catching my heart in my throat.

"I love your eyes," I blurt out.

"I hate them. They're a freak of genetics, make me look just like..."

I cut him off with a hand on his lips. "You, Twiz. When I look at them, I just see you."

With that, he lowers his mouth slanted over mine and kisses me with a fierceness that I don't think he's ever used before. It's not pretty, or romantic. The chill in the fall air makes both our noses run as our teeth clash. My head presses against the hard frame of the truck until I feel one of his hands slip itself between. His other hand is cold as it finds entry at the bottom of my sweater and travels up my side, making my skin break out in goosebumps.

He stops for a moment, his breath in pants that fog the space between us.

"I think I started to fall when you handed me a pair of clippers, but I know that I've loved you since that first run. No matter how hard I tried not to. Erika McNeil. I. Love. You."

His eyes are glued to mine until I close the distance between us again and this time, there's no break, not when his hand finishes its journey up and slowly strokes me with his thumb, or when I feel his excitement pressed against my belly.

It's the sound of a truck passing on the highway behind me that gets our attention.

"We need to go before I get us arrested," he mumbles to my lips, and with one more kiss, straightens my sweater and leads me back to my seat, leaning across to buckle me in and closing the door before climbing in on his side.

"Better?" He smirks.

"It'll do for now," I say, and he just barks a laugh.

"I've got all the time in the world, Hellcat."

EPILOGUE

TWIZ

ELEVEN MONTHS LATER

I'll never get over how much warmer it still is here in Ottawa compared to the already below freezing nights in Edmonton. The race route is lined deep with cheering spectators and excited family and friends of the racers, and we make our way the last kilometer of our third race together. This time, it's the Canadian Army Run.

Erika is beside me, probably in better shape than I am as we come around the last bend, her long legs flexing her well-earned muscles for the twenty-first kilometer of the run. No matter how often I look at her, she never stops taking my breath away.

That could also be the run, keeping up with this girl is a challenge I look forward to every day.

We pass the finish together and slow to a walk. She takes my hand and I let her, even as we walk to a shiny-faced private who puts dog tag-shaped finishing medals around both our necks. As we wander to a spot near the grass, I watch Erika finger hers, turning it over in her hand before letting it fall against her t-

231

shirt. We're both wearing "Louise's Gym" t-shirts, hers is pink and mine is olive drab.

Having the shirts before the opening was her idea as a form of advertising, and since our doors open next month with her as the general manager, she gets to make those decisions anyways. I still have a while longer before my last day in the military, but together, we used the money from the sale of my dad's land to buy the space almost six months ago, and we've been fixing it up since then. Shane is one of the trainers I've hired, along with a bunch of veterans who are now fitness instructors or training to be. We're offering fitness classes, personal training but also most importantly, free self-defence classes for women. Erika even partnered us with local women's shelters to offer free memberships and classes. We're already pre-booked with so many clients interested in the idea of training with military veterans, we can more than cover it.

I've spent most of my time with Erika at her condo, and watching her come out of her shell was the inspiration I needed for my own battle. We've both been in counselling, Erika learning to heal from the trauma of her abuse, to let go of her misplaced shame, to make friends, to enjoy running for more than control over her body but instead for the challenge and the camaraderie and the health benefits. To remember that some days, it was okay to stay in bed, and to learn, really learn, that I loved her for more than her appearance. The few pounds she's put on since have only added to her appeal. She's happy, and that's way sexier than I would have understood even a year ago.

My own therapy will take time, no matter how much I wish it was an easy fix, it's never going to be. Three different medications later, a host of side effects and panic attacks and even more than a few nights where all I could do with Erika was hold her while my body betrayed me, I have more good days than not lately. I've worked up to saying entire paragraphs at group with the counsellor. More than anything, being able to picture my future has been the biggest step.

Seeing Erika in it, that part has made all the difference.

It's been an amazing ride, and even though I chose to let go of the career I've used to define me my whole life, I never imagined I'd find something that meant even more to me.

I only have one more step.

We came to Ottawa, not only to race but so Erika could visit her friend Megan. It gave me the chance to talk to my old commander, Major Lawson, who will be coming back to the unit pretty soon with a new Lieutenant Colonel title. I had spoken to her dad before I left, but with no real dad of my own to talk it over with, it was nice to let him in on my plans while the girls chatted. Now, I can see him on the ridge next to his tearful wife, and I'm even more sure this is exactly what I want to do.

When Erika looks back up from her stretch on the grass, she freezes to see me, on my knee in front of her. There's already a small crowd of race finishers and their families watching, but none of it matters.

"Erika McNeil, you are the most stubborn, most fearless, most headstrong, most amazing woman I've ever met. I can never repay you for the trust you've given me, or the way you love me. The best I can offer is that same love in return. Would you marry me, Hellcat?"

There are hundreds of people milling around and almost all of them have realized what's happening now, but I don't hear a word. I see only her. She doesn't cover her face or squeal or burst into tears like every other proposal I've ever seen. She puts her hand out to me and pulls me to my feet, the small, princess-cut diamond with white gold band between us as she looks me face to face.

"Over and over, Twiz. Over and over for the rest of our lives."

I'm pretty sure everyone around us cheers and claps, but the only other person in my world at that moment is her, and she said yes. I crush the almost-forgotten ring box between us with the fierceness in my kiss.

Somehow, with all these people three thousand kilometers away from where we live, my home was just built right in front of me.

SNEAK PEEK

BROKEN HOME

The first thing I notice when I come to is how cold it is. Our house is always warm, hot even. Years of sleeping in the worst conditions means I hate sleeping in the cold.

It wakes me with a start. I assume I must be in the field, in a tent, or even under the stars. The ground under me is hard, and I have no blanket covering me.

Then I open my eyes, and I remember.

"I'm not doing this anymore, Jeremy."

There was a finality to it that time, more than all the times in the years before. She had said that sentence over and over. She'd left me more times than I even remembered. But that time, that time it felt true.

"C'mon, Love. You don't mean that. It's just a rough go, we'll be fine. I have a job now, and I'll cut back on the beer, right? That's what you want? We can get on, Love, just need a little while..."

It had been then I'd noticed the packed bags. Not just her big one, but the smaller ones next to it. The sight of them had made my blood run cold.

She'd left so many times.

She'd never packed a bag.

*"It's not a rough go, Jeremy. It's a rough... it's a rough **life**. And I can't do it anymore."*

I went to reach for her, but I was swaying on my feet. Too much beer. Too much hurt.

I yelled. I don't even know what I said. Something hurtful. Something cruel, probably.

Then there was the plaster on my hand.

In my hand.

Deep in the skin of my knuckles.

I flex them now, and the pain shoots up my arm. Caked blood cracks as the skin moves under it, the smell of copper mixing with the bleached-out smell of the room around me.

It hurts.

I hurt.

I hurt her.

"I'm leaving, Jeremy. You need help but not from me. Not anymore. I'm leaving."

"Deb, you don't want to leave..."

"I DO!" She looks at me, broken, then takes a deep breath and the certainty in her eyes undoes me.

"There's someone else, Jer. I'm sorry. Please, let us go. Get help but let us go."

Every part of me aches as I sit up. I hear my knees crack as I throw them over the side of the bench. Nausea pitches in my gut, and I double over, with my head between my knees. I keep my eyes open, staring at the socks on my feet, wondering abstractly where my shoes are, willing myself to focus on that. If I close them, I can still see her.

"Deb! Deb, don't do this!"

She's crying. Who made her cry? Did I make her cry? Rage blinds my vision as I see the kids in the backseat of the car. They're staring at me with tears running down their face. I move towards them. I just want to hug them, hold them, tuck them in bed, here, with me.

"Stop, Jeremy. Just let us go."

When she turns, I see the plaster in her hair. It matches my fist, and I see a flash of my hand as it punches through the drywall next to her tear-streaked face that's frozen in fear.

I did this.

"Let us go, you asshole! Please, just let us go."

I did this.

I stand frozen, eyes riveted to the white flakes in her tangled black hair, as she throws the last bag in and opens the driver's door.

"When... When will you be back?"

My voice is cracked and broken, like the plaster, and just as irreparable.

She just shakes her head at me, and it causes a piece of the white rock to fall to her shoulder.

"Just let us go, Jeremy."

I screw my eyes shut, covering my face with my hands. I hear a deep moan that sounds like it comes from a wounded animal somewhere. It's not until I open my eyes again that I realize it came from me. My stomach is rolling inside me, attempting to banish any of the liquid poison that might be lingering inside. My mouth waters, and I swallow hard, breathing deeply to try to keep it down.

"Jeremy Finnamore?" a loud voice calls out, accompanied by the metallic clank of the locks.

I look down at the hard, cement bench I am lying on, the white toilet in the corner, the drain in the middle of the floor.

"Sir," I croak out, sounding like a soldier, albeit a broken one, responding more out of instinct than understanding.

"On your feet. Let's get you sorted out."

Stepping into view is a man who looks smaller than the voice makes it sound, a pressed uniform on that makes him look as sterile as the holding cell I've found myself in.

I stand, swaying a little on my feet, my head a rush. The door opens, and the officer enters, his handcuffs in his grip, barely contained look of disgust on his face.

"Just let us go, Jeremy."

The last piece of plaster falls from her hair and onto the ground behind her.

I did this.

MORE BY KIM MILLS

THE WAY HOME SERIES

All The Way Home *(Tavish and Juliette)*
Fight For Home *(Mark and Megan)*
Broken Home *(Jeremy and Jordyn)*

COMING SOON

The Long Way Home *(Bill and Patricia)*
Carry Me Home *(Matt and Sarah)*

THE WHAT I NEED SERIES

Harder Than It Should Be *(Lincoln and Abby)*

DEAR READER

Twiz, Erika, and Jordyn's story, along with all of the Way Home series, is fiction, but the realities of PTSD, domestic violence, and sexual assault is not. I hope that the characters I wrote portrayed the struggle and profound strength of those who are dealing with these issues. You are not alone.

If you are hurting, I encourage you, most of all, to reach out to the support network in front of you. Whether it's family, friends, or your military community, let someone in. Finding solid ground again is just that much easier when you're not out their flailing on your own.

If you don't know where to turn, there are resources out there for you. Here are just a few.

(Canada) The Member Assistance Program

(24/71-800-567-5803

(Canada) Assaulted Women's Help Line (24/7)

1-866-863-0511

(USA) MILITARY ONESOURCE (24/7)
1-800-273-8255 and Press 1

(USA) RAINN (RAPE, ABUSE AND INCEST NATIONAL NETWORK)
24/7
1.800.656.4673

ACKNOWLEDGMENTS

I am here but by the grace of my God, and forever grateful that His mercies are new each morning. I never fail to need them. To my husband: these past couple of years would have challenged any man, and the way you stepped up was nothing short of amazing. I could accomplish nothing without your voice and your leadership. Almost twenty-five years later, you still keep me standing.

My kids, you've adapted to a mom who's up all night writing and not by acting out, but by letting me sleep and bringing me coffee when you leave for school. I don't know how you've ended up so amazing, but you are.

For everyone that reads *She is Fierce*. The blog, the articles, the travel, the book… It's all yours. It amazes me every single day that you are all following along on this journey. My story is your story. Thank you for your support, and for those times you trust me with your voice.

For my Beta Readers, you help me mold these characters into who they were meant to be, and I couldn't do this without you. For everyone part of the Way Home Reader's Group, you guys are the best. Thank you for your comments, suggestions, encouragement, and support.

As always, I'm the spouse of a cocky armoured soldier, who wrote a book about a group of cocky infantry soldiers. I'm more than grateful for the calls that are still answered when I have questions at all hours. To all our military family who have put up with my writing over the years, I will continue always to show my appreciation the way I know you'd want it: By keeping your damn name out of it.

ABOUT THE AUTHOR

Run from Home is the third novel for writer Kim Mills, the author of the Canadian military family blog *She is Fierce*. Kim has been married to her high school sweetheart for over seventeen years and together they have three children. You can find the five of them, along with their dog Trooper, at home wherever the Army sends them.

You can find Kim on social media: